LIFE'S TUMULTUOUS PARTY

Reduced to its Essential Partycycles

MARVIN COHEN

Edited by Colin Myers

Set in Mrs Eaves XL with LaTeX.

ISBN: 978-1-944697-87-7 (paperback)
ISBN: 978-1-944697-88-4 (ebook)
Library of Congress Control Number: 2019951690

Sagging Meniscus Press
Montclair, New Jersey
saggingmeniscus.com

Parts of this book have appeared previously in:

- *Ambit* #88, 1982 (ed. Martin Bax)
- *Book Forum* vol. V/#4, 1981 (ed. Marshall Hayes)
- *Harper's & Queen*, December 1979
- *Inspired by Drink*, 1988 (ed. Joan & John Digby)
- *New Directions in Prose and Poetry* #23, 1971 (ed. James Laughlin)
- *Vogue (UK)*, December 1970
- *International Herald Tribune*, September 6th 1980
- *Sadness Corrected*, Sagging Meniscus Press, 2019

A MARVIN COHEN INVITATION

THIS IS A BOOK ABOUT PARTIES, written by a party expert: not a party-giver, but a party-goer—a person, for whom at one time, parties were essential for survival, of both body and soul.

Marvin Cohen was born in Brooklyn in 1931. A lifelong Yankees fan, he still plays softball. He started studying art at Cooper Union, but left after finding himself writing rather than doing his assignments.

A full-time literary career was frustrated by having to live, leading to a wide range of jobs, including: mink farmer; seaman on an oil-tanker bound for Cuba; summer-camp counsellor; Post Office employee; and worker in a "pretty smelly" doll factory. "I have had serious and boring jobs in the past that have helped me to write. I have been fired by most of my previous bosses as they perceived boredom." *[Kensington Post, February 20th 1981]*

Marvin's first publication was a poem in the small press magazine *Folder #3, 1955,* his next in the seminal anthology: *The Beat Scene, 1960* (ed. Elias Wilentz) alongside Ginsberg and Kerouac. However, Marvin says (with a grimace) that he was never a "beat" but he was (with a grin) an "intellectual."

Not making much of an impact in Manhattan, in October 1965, Marvin visited London: "They loved me because I was a magnificently unique example of an unpatriotic American. I was loved, pampered, indulged. Anybody who wasn't impressed by me in England was still in a state of shock over the loss of the Indian empire. I was invited to a moated castle in which regicides resided. I slept in the same bed that Harold Wilson *[former U.K. Prime Minister]* and his wife slept in . . . I got a hearing aid free from the National Health Service. I infiltrated all the concentric and eccentric literary circles in London. The holes in my jacket sleeves were from rubbing elbows with the corresponding bones of the English literary nobility . . ." *[Books, April 1968]*

Nonetheless, writing was "often a running war with poverty. Imagine having 75 part-time jobs and sacked from half of them. Solving the problem of survival is no easy trick. I pull in my belt, live in a railroad flat on the Lower East Side, and live on as little as I can. We live in a tribal, global world, where even countries are interdependent. Some people are defensive and hypocritical about the uses to which they put other people; a deception I certainly can't afford." In the past he has admitted to wearing only donated clothes and to smiling "with satisfaction 'n getting all giddy when I acquire a new friend my size." (Not so easy since Marvin is a big-framed 6'4"!).

And so to parties. In his prime, Marvin was renown for popping in on friends before dinner and arriving first at parties to devour the buffet before the other guests turned up. In the UK, Marvin attended parties with the likes of Francis Bacon, Jean Shrimpton and B.S. Johnson. Julia Lacy's *International Herald Tribune* interview with Marvin (reprinted here) further details Marvin's party pomp. Others have said of Marvin and his survival mechanisms:

— "Just as crocodiles need birds to come clean their teeth, so Marvin knows large houses need people to come live in them. Instinctively he knows this. It's symbiotic." (David Evers, London host.)
— "He's very un-English. Funny, with the calculating naivete of modern primitive artists. He says what nobody would dream of saying, makes things happen, and is affectionate." (Hattie Waugh, daughter of Evelyn.)
— "The key to his style of writing as well as his style of being is that he speaks the way most people just think. People either love Marvin or can't stand him. They can't stand that kind of honesty." (Edie Coulson, hostess.)
— "Marvin never remembers names so at parties he'll come up and say something like, 'See that man. I call him the shallow

man or the unwelcome man.' And he's always right. Whenever I see him at a party, I know I have someone to listen to."
(William Cole, New York book critic.)

— "I knew right away when Marvin walked in the door that
he was a loner because he was carrying a suitcase and he
wasn't going anywhere. 'Some loners,' Marvin says, 'have to
carry shopping bags around just to hold on to something of
the world.' But with Marvin, it's a whole suitcase, full of his
own novels, short stories, poems and fables . . . Last summer
they kept looking round at parties in Manhattan expecting
to see Marvin march in—Marvin does not sneak in, his gate-
crashing technique is more like the SAS but he was among the
missing. He was in London . . . crashing parties and watching
cricket . . ." (Stanley Reynolds, author and journalist.) Note:
He was also attempting to play cricket; a tail-end batsman
and non-bowler.

Over a hundred magazine and anthology contributions have
followed; from the internationally regarded (e.g. *Ambit*, *Harpers
Bazaar*, *Hudson Review*, *New Directions*, and *The Transatlantic Review*) to local newspapers (*Bay News*, *The Villager*, etc.) and small,
almost samizdat, publications (such as: *Ararat Quarterly*, *Fire Exit*,
Fly By Night, *Hyn Quarterly*, and *Tamarind*). Marvin also turned his
hand to writing plays and shorter dramatic pieces, performed
at Joseph Papp's Public Theater, the Edinburgh Fringe and on
many other stages.

By 1982, Marvin had published six collections of short
pieces (stories, dialogues and essays), two novels, and perhaps
the definitive work on the meaning of baseball. You could own
these books just for the exuberance of their titles:

— *Dialogues*, 1967
— *The Self-Devoted Friend*, 1967
— *The Monday Rhetoric of the Love Club and Other Parables*, 1973

- *Baseball the Beautiful: Decoding the Diamond*, 1974
  (expanded edition with originally intended title: *Baseball as Metaphysics*, 2017)
- *Fables at Life's Expense*, 1975
- *Others, Including Morstive Sternbump*, 1976
- *The Inconvenience of Living and Other Acts of Folly*, 1977
- *How the Snake Emerged from the Bamboo Pole but Man Emerged from Both*, 1978
- *Aesthetics in Life and Art, Existence in Function and Essence and Whatever Else is Important Too*, 1982

and here are two titles that were advertised but never saw print:

- *The Hard Life of a Stone and Other Thoughts*, 1975
- *The Department Store of Global Confinement & Other Entireties*, 1978

Alas, though much critical acclaim ensued (reaping a Yaddo fellowship), it was not enough to give Marvin the fame he cherishes. Thence a drift into a less fraught existence: a loving marriage to the lovely Candace Watt (an editor, initially approached at a party because she might help him sell his work); and teaching adult education, including "Psychology and Philosophy of Humour" at Cooper Union and Hofstra University, and "Creative Writing" at Hofstra, CCNY and the New School. Unfortunately, you've missed your chance, as his last taught course was in 2009.

Of his approach to teaching, Marvin has written: "The students do whatever they want and then I give them a reaction. I had to be self-taught. It was tough for me in school. I couldn't hear so well, and I lived in a dream world to escape from the ruthless world of conformity and cruelty against somebody as handicapped as I was. I was sort of eccentric. It's easy for a hard-of-hearing person to become eccentric by stepping out of the rhythm of his society." *[The Listener, November 8 1973]*

Then followed a publication hiatus, retirement, and, more recently, a renaissance: reprints of his short piece collections into one volume, *How to Outhink a Wall*, by Verbivoracious Press; reprints of his longer works by Tough Poets Press; two novels, and two collections of recent prose and poetry (on aging, friendship, loving and living) published by Sagging Meniscus Press.

And now this collection: first mooted in 1981, combining unanthologized magazine pieces, works from Marvin's big box of unpublished typescripts, and a scattering of newer pieces. It could have been longer, but some potential episodes left to become interested parties in Marvin's published novels.

Of his own work, Marvin has said:

"Perhaps half or a third of the books I ever read have influenced my own work; especially James Joyce, Kafka, Henry James, some of the French surrealists like Henri Michaux, William Faulkner, and the 18th-Century English prose style; many unconscious influences have been at work, too.

"My work has been influenced by such personal factors as my rather isolated Brooklyn childhood, my semi-deafness from the age of three; my interests in Major League baseball, art, and music; early abortive love life, poverty, the cosmos of New York City, travelings and tattered abundance of jobs, and idlenesses. However, my work hardly ever touches *literally* on events, being rather surrealistically abstract." *[Monk's Pond #4, 1981, ed. Thomas Merton]*

"I couldn't write the sort of stuff *most people* like if my life depended on it." *[From Mt St Angelo, 1984, ed. William Smart]*

And of this book: Marvin has the pleasure to invite you to read it in whichever order takes your fancy.

—*Colin Myers*

Table of Participation

LIFE'S
TUMULTUOUS
PARTY

WHY PARTIES?

Being in groups changes people. Groups aren't predictable. Unforeseen moods may condition them. Each party forms itself to be a unique entity. It clusters itself from separate individuals into a surprisingly coherent mood-collective comprising many different consciousnesses that are all affected to a mutual extent by the joint orchestration they play into and from. Each party—on all the gradations from better to worse—is an exclusive, finite universe of its own character, packed into a duration from which it becomes unwound, freeing itself from its own binding and momentary essence. We were huddled together, we guests, or however apart: cells to a short-lived organism. Then the cells scatter, and the organism collapses dead on its empty site, like a balloon loosened of the well-dressed molecules of air (or casually attired) which pumped it shining into a rounded being catching scintillating glints of light on the taut surface artifice.

Parties are laboratories or libraries for the latest research into social fashion, where configurations or constellations are formed with breathless brevity, chalked on the much-erased blackboard of history, complete with audible chatter and gossip, and the cunning patterns of courtship (brief-term seductions) along with negotiations on a scheme of career, deals in the hazards of advancement in the lines of making a reputation and a living in a field of fruitful endeavor taking a special position that confers status and flexible maneuver. Deals are tentative, appointments hinted at, arrangements skirted into or flirted at, in the great interplay of play and work on an open private spectacle or subtle public secret worked at, worked out, brought about, to come into play. Parties are informal meetings of a definite business nature: trade conventions, commercial semi-rituals, a private free-for-all for what the market can bear in the lot of individual chancing.

A party is a stock exchange in human fortunes, venture brought to the risk, bartering securities, gambling little or much in the stray toss of opportunities staked in caution or taken on a plunging impulse that dares to transact the unknown on the calculated hope for a shift and boost in the enterprise of one's lot, pulling away and surveying the next move—while retaining one's reserves and clutching tight to the entrenched virtues and stale advantages from which one has gained such vantage as perches prospectively on change while holding fast to the sure stock of long-attained assets.

A person at a party is fixed by the circumstance of that party to a socially environmental set of conditions, within the framework of which he's "free" to talk and generally behave in the specific expression of "himself," in contrast to the rest of the group, from which he stands out but in which he remains submerged, since his individuality is understood in terms of "participating and being part of." A party guest (or crasher) is a member of that party. It's a temporary membership, soon to be sundered. While *of* the party, the person performs himself by comparison with his fellows with whom he shares the mass conditions of the event: the common pool of intoxication, mingled voices, expelled air, hovering above.

RATIONALIZATIONS OF THE PARTY ADDICT, WHEN CRITICALLY QUERIED BY ADVOCATES OF SOCIAL "MODERATENESS"

"Parties are my ballpark, my arena, my Coliseum, my stock market, and my social parachute jump. A party means an alarm is going off in the social beehive. Lives crisscrossing. I like to dissect the lives that bisect.

"I need to feel part and parcel of the human community, in the warm huddling of my fellow kind against a cold, unconcerned universe of impersonal distances, interstellar remoteness, and mortality's incessant inner tick.

"I scream that I'm going to be dead—but I scream it silently. Then I muffle my fear, blunt my horror, smother my terror, in the tribal blur of alcoholic chatter, dancing a shuffling rhythm around the makeshift campfire of the lonely fabricated temporary togetherness. We link metaphoric arms, touch metaphoric hands, communicate by signals and grunts. The comforting blaze is at hand. Drinks, communion, the bond of the occasion. Joined by the fragile threads of our numbered massive body."

The addict further confesses, to his imaginary audience which he endows with the courtesy of a deferential attentiveness and rather awed respect for his bravely summoned words:

"How did I begin this dreadful salvation of my addiction? Loneliness drove me to party after party. At parties I found love, or its mirage. And the heady wine of companionship, friendship. Alternating with a persisting curse of feeling incurably uncompoundable, was a growing facility in the art of 'meeting people.'

" 'Inherently uncompoundable,' was my self-diagnosis. Loneliness stubbornly inbuilt to outbrave all the rosy onslaughts of 'love.'

"Parties were for making conquests or getting rejected. They were to confirm loneliness by making the conquests spurious and the rejections almost comically chronic.

"Parties were: to sight glory, only to have it crumble. Romance was kindled at the slightest 'realistic' provocation of a 'soulful' conversation flirtatiously entered but burst into disillusionment either that night or in a week or a month. Parties offered and withdrew love with the abundance of an empty handful of hope and the pang of an endless quest.

"The longing for love is so keen that even when you *have* it you go on looking for it at the next party. It's the soul's tapeworm that aches us into a plenitude's starvation and having's not-having."

The addict's confession covers self-pity over with grim bitterness. Now he's too far in to stop coyly short with murky self-analysis:

"The lonesome loner, ever out of rhythm, cut off, out of step. How can you avoid feeling left out, when people aren't exactly falling all over themselves to invite you in includingly?

"I needed something to hold on to—as mine, my own. Bag ladies or bag men accumulate some personal junk to hold on to—chunks of the real outside world, that they collected and by acquisition incorporated onto their very selves, their hoarded capital: concrete commodity wealth.

"I'm a mild case compared to them. I'm just driven to parties."

❄

The addict paused. He remembered that he wasn't supposed to be lonely anymore. He'd forfeited that solemn birthright by having failed outright in his great loneliness crusade. He had a steady girlfriend, they lived together in a marriage, their bond had grown to be lasting. That lost him the right to moan. He needed a new tack to take, in defensive rationalization of his un-interrupted partygoing in spite of the loss of loneliness's dark despairing lonely romantic excuse. He was happily paired off. Yet he still craved company.

"Now, I'm blessed with a girlfriend. Desperation is done. But I need to observe people. People are variations and versions of myself. I'm their scholar. They're specimens of my endless study—they're my aggravation and my love, obsessively both at once, for their truth is only partial and never revealed. They're my fascination, and my sickness.

"Parties are a living library for me. They're moving and breathing galleries like a collection of books proclaiming themselves in capsule.

"Talking with people is more instantaneous than even the vivid abstraction of reading books. How many thousands of pages can one person be worth, when you're really 'interchanging' with him?

"I'm not just a silly social butterfly on the make. I'm a people-specialist.

"I won't always be here on earth in this living state. While I am, however, I want to feel ties—however glowing or trivial—with my fellow beings in passage.

"To steep myself inside the pulse, throb, and beat of a multiple human nature, with their opening faces and their concealing clothing, I attend—sometimes uninvited—parties.

"Social life's semi-strife, the rough and tumble and knocking about, offering occasional enlightenments but normally only slightly ruffled obscurities, is a sometime way of life. To romp in the refined wildness, the subdued uninhibitedness, the stylized mystery of parties, is to sometimes come away with a glitter of findings—people's piths, glimpsed essentially through the fractured fragmentariness of scattered addressing and attitudes of shock-absorbent accidents in the twirl of confrontation, easing off, collision, or coming to grip."

The addict shows that party-going is to be a peopleizer. To be a people-addict is to be a partyizer. He's a participating observer. He learns to know the human soul.

"Some nice people turn lousy, some rotten people come out okay, under the certain strenuous relaxed urgency that parties can provide. We key in on old characteristics undergoing novel transformations in more or less civilized settings that are open arenas for looking while under someone else's gaze; for listening while being overheard yourself, in the interplay of objects and subjects, the conditioned jungle of our exchanges: standards broken in being set up.

"Amid the beaming palsy-walsy of one party, we come up with a benign sparkle. But when aggressive, hostile flack holds its sway, bad growls come guttering out."

He feels guilty about maybe being accused of frivolity. After all, he works hard—in the day. He rationalizes party-going, in line with getting work done.

"But I do a lot of solitary work which requires solitude to get it done. Paradoxically, parties can assist my solitude-needing system. There, I can get my dose of people all in a lump. In the day I do my work. Then, concentrated people in the night—a smorgasbord payoff for enduring earlier privation, rather than the diluted idleness of day-long semi-snacking.

"At parties I fill my ears with an abounding medley-bedlam of language. I gather a headful of noisy meanings split up from the central din.

"I fill myself with the matrix and fabric of human voices in the yapping cacophony of social intercourse. Thousands of 'thou's into the middle of my 'me.' They merge into my mobile muse, collecting at rife random, in the selective shuffle of chanced-upon opportunities or seized-upon prey."

He concludes his self-addiction-defense. Being at a party is like being in the world—you're there. Make, then, the most of the present thing.

"If you find yourself at a party where you weren't invited, you may as well avail yourself—being there—of what's there. I didn't ask to be born—but as I'm here, it's too tempting not to take advantage of it. Why lose out, once you're on to a good thing?"

The addict stops rationalizing. Sufficient unto the life is the party thereof: Since we're each a party to the larger party of life itself, many doors into crowded rooms where people enjoy and contemplate their contemporaries—or hate them, can't bear them, but suffer them, mixed in a misery of those co-mortal selves confined in rooms and apartments of their own shared choosing, the silence and noisy drinking of people bobbing up and down in the same landed boats—prisons by choice,

chapels or temples, privileged places, or spaces sacredly pro-
faned, where co-sufferers compare notes and exchange views
from separate universes that bear in on the choked simultaneity of their joint attendance that bears the solemn unanimity of
their witness. Each testifies, reports. It's boiled down to their
central oneness.

THE CHILDREN'S RAINY AFTERNOON TEA PARTY

"A precocious little boy said he'd like to be a walking fish . . ."

Like a basket of mushrooms gathered from (naturally) a mushroom forest, the children were all gathered in out of a rainy afternoon in a snug large apartment room to have a tea party and talk. They fumbled around on various topics fishing for one with a general interest. They wanted the cosy camaraderie of all dwelling on the same thing. After some brutal trials, they settled on that strange ethereal subject, reincarnation. One bright little girl said that in her next life she would like to be a flying lion who looked like the average lion but with the addition of wings. She had made a sensation, for everyone gasped.

A precocious little boy said he'd like to be a walking fish with a pair of air-breathing lungs that would adapt him to any land life including a desert's.

"Then he wouldn't be a fish any more, strictly speaking," a literalist perked up, revealing the inherent destructiveness of criticism. But the criticised remained undaunted, stubborn to the end. That's the way little children have, of protecting their insights—for some. Others give in, lose out, and join herd thinking.

That little altercation subdued, and with plenty of ice-cream and cake being consumed for the benefit of giving the tea its extra function of having something to wash down, the little children romped on, down the valleys of conversation, through the corridors of mystery. A studious little boy remarked how in his next metamorphosis he would like to jump backwards into being his father. Later on in that new life, he would give birth to his very self—via, of course, his wife-mother. This intrigued the children no end. They contemplated the rudiments of an Oedipus Complex, without knowing it.

Luckily, no adult was present. The "hosts" were a brother and sister whose parents were both away and wouldn't be back for hours. So the apartment belonged to the children. Their gaiety rose.

"In my next metamorphosis," said a puckish little rascal with a crooked and naughty little grin that showed he liked to get away with mischief, "I want to be all of you at once," motioning to everyone there assembled. "After all," he continued, owing a slight explanation to somewhat clarify the perplexity which his remark had spread among the little heads he had implicated into his scheme for a composite future life for his own little self, "the world is conducted in groups these days. The tribal, the communal, instead of the individual, are being increasingly stressed. Pressure is being brought to bear on each one of us to belong and conform to however small a mass. So why not me too? In my next life I'll incarnate into all of your lives as you are now; you'll all be dead then, of course; but I'll incorporate all your simple identities into one all-inclusive one, which shall be me—not the me of today, but the me of next life. I hope I'm not befuddling anyone?" he asked, with apprehensive courtesy. He received a warm response. Everyone welcomed the idea of being preserved in some new form. If *this* boy would carry them, their lives would be perpetuated, or their spirits. That would be marvellous. It would give immortality a head start.

A lot of buzzing ensued, cross-hatcheries of debate and some amiable controversy. Ideas were loose and being exchanged. It was like an open market place, and a flow of commerce, brisk trading between heads. That showed how beneficial an assemblage could be, especially in those early formative years, when learning could be so vivid. Each life was getting enriched. The afternoon indoors tea party was a smashing success for its social intention; the rain ought secretly to be thanked, for, had the day been fair, the children would have been playing outside, in scattered groups, all their games of convention and innovation. That was the obvious likelihood had the sun been out. But *this* way, ideas were nourished on an intimate and intellectual level. God must have *planned* that rain. Or if not God, then praise the skies, which decide such matters.

Now a little girl chirped up who hadn't spoken before. She was a cute and innocent little thing, wearing a beribboned pigtail that extended far below the nape.

She said: "In my new incarnation I intend to be a boy. That will balance out my awareness, which is weighed down in the onesidedness of my being currently always a girl and only that. It will open up a new vision, subjectively speaking, with which to interpret the business of life. Being a girl and only that is such a narrow business! My next life will give it an opposite viewpoint to be compared with. Much learning is by way of contrast, like opposites. And what's so polar as the two mutually exclusive genders! From whence comes romance, love and sex; as well as plenty of neurosis.

"So in my new life I'll be a boy and see how the other half lives. The illumination will round me out and so broaden my horizons that I'll transcend sex altogether!"

This speech received some gentle applause. But a member of the audience who hadn't spoken before—a boy, by identity— had a criticism to make. His objection took the form of a scientific factual accuracy scruple. Reduced to their essentials, his points came down to this: "Between one incarnation and the next, the consciousness of the first life is lost: not even a dim recollection is retained in the succeeding life of the one 'graduated' from. We begin all over from scratch. So you, a girl, who expect to *increase* your knowledge of human life through being a boy in the next life—you're operating on a mistaken assumption, it's my duty, I'm afraid, to inform you. Yes, you might well become a boy in your new life. But you will have entirely forgotten what you ever were in the present one. So it won't do you any good in the future that you're a girl *now*. You'll be ignorant of everything in your current phase."

But the girl had a ready retort to defend herself with. Everyone was fascinated as she effectively argued; "The diary that I'm writing now, in my capacity as a girl, I'll continue making entries in, all through my remaining life as a woman, demonstrating every vicissitude in a total life feminine. I'll keep this diary always by my side, never failing to carry it about with me, like an acquired appendage, an extra arm. Except that it won't really *be* me. It'll be a thing outside of me, an object in itself. When I die and fly between metamorphoses toward the designation of my new incarnation of beginning life as a boy with a manly destiny—I'll be carrying this diary with me, *physically*, in my astral travel through the mystic region between this life and the next. When I land into my new life, I'll have it with me as a decisive testimonial, memento, accurate record—of me in *this* life, in being the girl I am and the subsequent woman phase. I'll have the evidence and study it—what it means to have been what I am in this life. It'll have *my* name, and *my* handwriting—and for proof, *my* fingerprints. That will bind me over in a bridge to connect with the further, and male, bank. It will serve as the transition link. It will be a great reminder, an archive of previous history, the museum of a predecessor, the library-witness. And as a man I'll become acquainted with the girl I am today."

"Well spoken," her critic objected, "but it'll do you no good. This diary, being only physical, is due to be lost in transit. If that disturbs you and destroys your premise—dashes your hopes as well—I'm sorry. Veracity obliges me to correct your illusion. Between incarnations, no physical property—whether of the human person's flesh or of any utensil or effect—may be conveyed. 'You can't take it with you' pertains not just to money or a savings account but to that diary as well. Even if it's a literary classic and will be read forever, like Pepys' masterpiece that has long survived. Only *other people* will be reading it. In fact, the man you'll be in your next incarnation may very well read it if he comes across it in a published edition. But he'll never know—alas, never—that the author, the late author, you, were the direct previous incarnation he had migrated from in his solar transformation. It sounds pathetic, tragic, but it can't be helped. A definite barrier or divider of complete oblivion will separate your next being from the current one—with nothing in between to dimly echo or link, or conduct, or convey, or transport. Bang, you'll be dead, Bang, there'll be a new life. But the you of today won't be in it; it'll be another you. And between the you's—no use. The borders hold, the margins keep each other out, mutually exclusive. Sorry to spoil your plans—I hope you'll sober up now. You'll think better of such a crackpot idea. You'll accept your fate. And do your roaming, unmindful of whence you came."

The girl was sobbing. Her afternoon was ruined. It rained all the way into night. Home came the parents; and the guests of their son and daughter all had to leave. The afternoon had been illuminating—but sad as well. The various children went home in scattered destinations, each clutching to his own current identity. This life could be concentrated on, for there was so much of it left. When it was nearly spent, later, thought could be given to the "Where do we go from here?" As yet, there's a whole development to cultivate, as one's own self, with the given body to hold it. To hold it for so long. When the hold gets tenuous—what next? By then they'll be ancient—some even dead already and in new guise. With a different self? Another soul? Or only a changed body form, containing the same kernel? The problem changes with age. Death may not solve it. The problem may always exist.

Was their appetite for dinner ruined by all that cake and ice-cream? That's the more immediate concern. The next day would be fair.

THE BOLD EXPANSION OF THE SNEAKER-IN

You heard about the party from the indirect buzz of rumor in passing; then hustled to pin down precisely the time, address, and occasion and to reckon the estimate of who would be there in what casual-or-not attire, calculate the likelihood of the atmosphere, spirit, duration, the 'feel' of that party—all in advance. What food and drink would there be? Would there be security precautions at the gate, the assessing eye of a list-bearing, in-the-know assistant to the host? The invitation card might even have to be shown. Even more formidable psychological barriers would lurk should you slip through the initial guard resistance.

Yet it all might be so easy. Put on the fitting clothes, and chance it. Arrive early, tense, watchful, inconspicuous, at an edge of the entrance scene, where you hover, fitfully, lurking tensely in the shadows, missing not a cue.

See the first people arrive, now they're admitted. If a group arrive, maybe you can fall in with them. Or you might see a genuinely invited guest whom you know, who'll wave you in under the wings of his spontaneously offered escort in sweeping through; it could even be genial.

Then, mingle casually. Dissipate your uneasy nerves with a rush of first drinks. Stealthily, approach the food table (if there is one—there might not be). Have a careless air. Converse, as if naturally. Mingle. You're there.

Act as though you solidly belong, finally. The hours pass. Your assurance has triumphed through. Once you've slipped in, then arrogance can gradually shine through. You're undistinguished from the true invited guest—having even outeaten (if given the material opportunity) and surely outdrunk him.

You took revenge—for being uninvited. You pillaged around, you ravaged the joint. You made some valuable social, business, careerist, sexual contacts, by the increasing assurance of aggression.

You made it into your own party. Grudgingly, you're among the last to leave. You were all brazenly amidst the throng. You compensated for the furtive approach, by guarded stealth, early outside the threshold.

The party became yours—a takeover. Centrally at its pivot, you coasted along, in the high festivity of unearned insolence.

You transformed the party. You became its occasion, its host, its celebrant. Welcome all those people. Be open-handed. Take them upon yourself. Bestow on them your generosity.

You came to take. You stay to give.

A PARTY AS A PERSON—OR A PERSON AS A WHOLE PARTY. FROM LOTS TO ONE UNIT. ONE UNIT *CONSTITUTES* ALL THE LOT. PEOPLE EXIST, VIA THE PERSON. IT STARTS WITH HIM. AND PANS OUT, TO A PARTY.

The party was in full fledge. It was really going on—as though it had a will of its own—as though the party were one person, in motion. But that's only a way of looking at it. And thereby, a way of describing it.

It takes lots of people, all together, to make a party. For what would a party be, without its people? Or a nation, for that matter? Or a city? Or a performance involving performers and audience? Or the whole world, for that matter?

Don't people have an actual hand in it—the world? Trees, rocks, water, birds and land and clouds are there too, of course. No self-respecting world would deem itself complete without all *those*, too.

But don't forget the people! They're real. They count—they stand up and do things.

People are the primary subject of novels—of plays—of art, and other things.

Without people, where would we all be?

So let's proclaim ourselves, us people, let's shout out a blast for ourselves, and herald our own trumpet, and make personal appearances as glowing testimonials. Our word counts. All of us!

Yes, but enough about people. What about a person? Don't forget *him*, too.

With all the fanfare, all the gala publicity, about people, people, more people—let single persons not be eclipsed by it, smothered and drowned out by it, rendered insignificant by it. Let not the mass of people deprive an individual person of his specific reality. Not abstractly, does he exist, and do what he does—but in the concrete. A person, in his thought. Wherein, the world rises, and life takes its place.

Life, in the specific. An individual. Who gives rise, to all the rest.

LIFE'S TUMULTUOUS PARTY

The party was raging at full speed. I was caught up in it. I talked my way through so many people! I was transferred in all directions from group or person to group or person, an interweaving of clusters, in conversational snatches.

The sparkling glasses contained—the glasses were sparkling with—intoxicating beverages.

Into mouths the beverages went, and issuing from those same mouths were words—those scatterments of ideas.

Social communication was being done all over the party. Social inter-communication, or intersocial communication. I was a moving part of all this—or a being-moved passivity.

I was a party to these goings-on: to the whole ensemble, that was the party. I was being moved about, and still further about.

I was really getting around. I made the rounds. With each soft colliding thud, I spent a minimal communication, extracted the same coin, and was on my way, in moving, all the way about, step by step, by stops and stages.

I was whirling about. Drinks were taking tolls. The drink went in, the words went out. The double-bladed function, all in the selfsame mouth. A useful tool, that.

The talking was filling the rooms, crowded with the bodies below all those opening mouths.

From people to people, I went. Making the party rounds. I took in people, they me. It was a drunken social evening, it got to be. And I by no means least. Nor worst, but cohesive, to the whole.

The whole of moving parts. The whole party, piece by piece, or by word units, all bulging with the bits.

We *were* the party. We made it up—as its components. No one was only a person. He was a party part. The drink and talk, in and out. Getting wilder. More animation, building up.

Louder. Toward the frenzy. The whole, taking over. The parts, swept up. As contributory bits, toward a massive event.

Getting out of hand. Drunker, wilder. Loud talk. There's anger. We can't control it. Nasty words, in bitter exchange. It's getting ugly. We must withdraw.

Or is it too late to retreat? There's confused scuffling. The exits are barred. Here we are, *in* it. This party. In short, our very world. Our only world, itself.

I'm dying to get out.

But that's the only way I *can* get out—through death, the courtesy of its solitude. I'm cut off, and caught up, in this raging world, disintegrating with violence.

In this, I'm stuck. I'm tightly held. To this permanent party. I entered, invited, as a guest. My host or hostess unknown. I leave only by death. I'm dying to leave.

I choose to stay. Life is out of hand. But I'm in it, all the way.

DISSOLVED IN THE THEM. NO MORE ME.

The party was working up a wild momentum. I was part of everybody else. As they would surge and roar, so would I, for in their larger will moved my smaller captive one.

The party was not just an evening social occasion. It now was a political body, organized to a despotic rule, totalitarian to all our time. We were stuck inside, as servile cells well mobilized to tyranny's call.

Where had my individuality gone? It was lost, and only consciousness remained, as a silent rebel. Bound to mob need, I feared the snuffing out of dear private thoughts as well. Then where would my lovely *self* go? The *me*, with my precious past plunged into peril.

The group had no need of my particularity. I'd be submerged, along its hard general lines. Melted away, ground down, to its simple principles, its undeviant doctrine. Subservience, with all my edges rubbed out, to the team's mission, and driven in its clear logic.

I was well lodged in there. Even protest grew fuzzy. Now I'm lost in its deep swell. Its truth compels. Its purity locks me close. I like it. The group is my will. My loyalty has defected to it. It sanctifies my conversion. I live with commitment. I'm made over, to their singularity-devouring collective. My peace is violent. Someone contributes, that was me. As a member only, the former me lies subdued. I *was* that person. Had I an "I" left, I'd refute that, too.

In me, the party burns. Its cause covers what my identity was. In its glorious crusade, I submit my will. To its single destiny, we grow a grand compound.

(A three-paragraphed title that knocks its gate down and totters out of control, approximating the rampaging text of its excessively out-of-bounds subject:)

THE PARTY THAT SWEPT ACROSS ITS LIMITS, AND GREW SWELLINGLY OUT OF HAND, IN A WILD SURGE OF HUMAN BULGE. IT WAS *TOO MUCH*. NEVER AGAIN!

BUT AT LEAST IT WASN'T DULL. NO, IT WASN'T DULL. IT PACKED TOO MUCH TERROR FOR THAT. IT GREW ALARMINGLY GIGANTIC. THE MOB PRESSED MY WILL DOWN. IT RAGED, TO AN OCEAN OF DRUNKEN EXCESS, THAT WILD PARTY. IT WAS TOO MUCH. IT LACKED THE TEMPERATE TOUCH.

BUT I CAN'T BEAR A *DULL* PARTY. NO, NOT THAT, PLEASE. *ANYTHING*, BUT THAT.

The party finally got too large for the apartment, so it had to spread out. The walls ran a danger of being pressed out, which might have caused buckling, then a collapse, leading the ceiling to fall down, people crushed, panicked, floor caving in, chaotic catastrophe. To avert which, the excess overflow oozed out the doors into halls, corridors, down elevators, into the nearest streets at hand, seized and consumed to popular demand.

The party size was getting out of hand. Someone forgot to limit the guest list. Word got around about the party, it slipped out and everyone, it seemed, got notified. It was the least exclusive party of an already bulging season. It kept growing, by more people arriving. The number of "guests," including uninvited crashers, was swollen beyond limits: but kept increasing far past the danger point. Hence, the overflow, into the night street. People were swilling from bottles there. Common human decency and courtesy were now beyond manageable proportions. The expansion grew antisocial, with surging unruliness all around, causing a rumbling of riots. Some party this turned out to be! Yes, some party! I'll never go there again! The frenzy of the mob had bit me there. I had no will of my own. It was overruled, at every turn. There was danger in the air. I could have suffocated, I swear!

Well, now I'm "safe and sound," all alone, at home. Why the party was a riot! It overlapped its boundaries, and kept pouring. The ones who were there didn't leave. The ones who weren't there arrived. What a crowd! What a tight crush! Then it overflowed, to halls, elevator, street. Humanity was thick and dense, that night, in its sheer bulk, with gruesome enlarging at a steady rate.

Everyone had to bring his own bottle. The liquor consumed that night! It could have filled a herd of elephants, a whole ranch of cattle, a whole farm of horse stables.

The police arrived, they cut through the mobs, divide people at their thickest points, where intimacy got swollen with red hostility. Public familiarity was breaking down private barriers.

Thank God I'm home now. Safe, alone. I can breathe here. Ah, I'm safe. I have privacy, at last. Dear sweet solitude. So roomy, so much space!

I was claustrophobic, at that party! I was losing all grips to my reason. It was terrifying, I was stifled. We were sweating out a nightmare—communally shared between unwilling brothers. Closely spread about. Tight, too close for comfort.

Oh, the drinking! We were all raving! We were senseless, but on our feet.

Just on our feet. Propped up, by the cordial neighbor.

Ah, alone! At last!

But lonely. Too lonely.

I want to go to a party. Not like *that*, of course. A little quieter, perhaps.

Yes, slightly toned down. A *modified* party. Tempered to manageable proportions. Mild, even subdued.

But not dull. No: some sparkle, some life.

But not surging out of hand. Not overpressing all limits!

The just-right party! Like the perfect wine! Sweet, yet bitter. Cold, yet light Hot, yet dark. Everything—yet something. Something refined, something nice. No bulging monster. No surging crowd. No brutal riot.

But not dull! I repeat, not dull! No, *anything* but that!

BEING FABULOUS

Some of the most fabulous people can be met at parties, where in fact some even *are* met, for there are so many people to choose from among, and somehow you can spot the fabulous ones, pick them out of a whole bunch, and instantly know who's fabulous, through the swift alarm of pure recognition.

But the question is this, when it comes down to it: Will those fabulous ones elect to know *you*? If they're fabulous, they're in demand. Power is theirs for choice. What will *they* see in *you*? Are *you*, your*self* fabulous?

Well, nobody is fabulous to *every*body. You'll be fabulous to some fabulous people, but not to most: not *nearly* to most.

How can you improve your fabulosity, to increase your fabulous conquests of the fabled and near-fabled?

Most people would *die* to know the answer to this. Just die—in order to be born again. To live—fabulous.

I'd make a fortune, if I knew. It would be the most popular ill-kept secret in the world. So popular, it would become over-exposed. It would lose its novelty value, its sacred mystery. It would lose everything—even itself. For with too many copiers, too many devotees, its force would ebb out of it, and the blood would turn to water, as available as the common air itself, and just as free and cheap, to all who owned lungs. Exclusivity must be guarded. That's why the rich, the aristocratic, the famous, the powerful, become so reserved, for they have so much to guard, to protect. To be fabulous is to be self-protective, to be in fact notoriously exclusive. The fabulous people are the justified, by necessity, snobs. Everybody's angling for them, laying traps, taking aim, putting out tempting enticements to snare some highly select favors from a few trickling moments of the fabulous lives of fabulous people.

Dark sunglasses, as an anonymity ploy, are worn sometimes by fabulous people. If non-fabulous people want to *appear* fabulous, to try to be mistaken for the fabulous, they ofttimes imitate superficial effects of *truly* fabulous people—like affecting the wearing of sunglasses (dark-tinted, of course) or a certain style of hairdo, clothingdo, shoedo. Sometimes it even works!

Some fabulous people are only so for only a time, then fall into eclipse, and wear the reduced status of people who were formerly fabulous. They sigh and sigh, pining with resignation, for their lost glory.

Some merely ordinary people suddenly zoom in ascension and become meteorically fabulous overnight; or *gradually* acquire their tremendous transformation. They appreciate the difference: importantly, so do their enviers, their spontaneously recruited overflowing armies of admirers. To be fabulous is to be *seen* as such. No one was ever fabulous on a deserted island. The acclaim by others, adoration, idolatry, are the true confirmation and endorsement by which fabulosity takes on its authentic merit.

I wish I were fabulous. I go to a party, hoping to be found fabulous by someone—especially by someone who's already fabulous herself. However, unfabulously, I'm ignored, too much. I wilt and wither, in the shade, outside of the sunny glint of being acknowledged fabulous, being stamped to the holy seal of privilege and esteem, as conferred by others with their look in their eye of spotting the real thing, the bona fide specimen, the actual within the veracity of its own truth, the fabulous as such, without a touch of the synthetic, without a speck of the dubious, but wholly contained within the generous license of being altogether fabulous—scorning all need for proof, not even bothering to bring along certificates of merit, raving testimonials, or other papered credentials of cravenly implicit petitionary appeal, the fawning publicity that bends to supplicate and becomes abjectly self-defeating.

Fabulous people *are* such, *as* such; no need to present a case or window-dress, or even indirectly to advertise. A fabulous person is simply a fabulous person, he *is*, without trying. Trying betrays false pretenses. To *be*, is to have an ease about it, casually indifferent to show. A fabulous person *is* fabulous: it's all of his state of being, at the intrinsic level of essence; and is identified as such, at once.

Oh to be fabulous! I try, but therein I fail. If I *were*, I wouldn't try, and I wouldn't fail. Oh, that I'm not it! I'm bitter in my deprivation. I hope, by miracle, to change all this, by conjuring a formula alchemically magic, invoking pagan gods and forbidden authorities, like Faust who blasphemed with expert Mephistophelean assistance. All I only want to be is fabulous, here below. Why is this not granted me? Whom, up high, have I offended? I come laden with gift-offerings to my redeemer, who shall enchant the spooks that be, to make my wish the genuine article, from vapor to solid. I *would* be fabulous. I *will* it. I try. I fail.

Let me not will or wish or want or would, nor try nor fail— but to *be* it. To be it, thus negating desire.

A want is a lack. Alas, alack, to want is a curse. Let me be, rather than want. To be fabulous, and be glad about it. To shine in the sheer fabulous, as a spectacle of numb awe to those who flock in witness or singly turn dumb, when in their presence I appear. I'll close my eyes, and count. I'll count to three; open my eyes—and behold—it's me! I'm fabulous.

The little daydream faded. I'm still not fabulous. Should I continue to hope? I don't want to court futility. I can't study the styles of those who *are* fabulous and be a genuine emulator and false copy of them. Either I'm it, or not. If not, in time maybe. But how? By some accidental miracle, or quiet growth? I hate whoever's fabulous. They're what *I* can't be. Why are they they, and me only me? Such odds degrade me. I'm puny, in my giant scale of "would be." I'm mocked by those I'm not.

Yet, *some* people think I'm fabulous. Even a few fabulous ones think so. Can I be part-time fabulous? A dilettante fabulous, a dabbler, the occasional Sunday fabulous? Or are you either are, or not? Are degrees permissible?

I'm not absolutely fabulous, but maybe relatively so. To *what*, relative? To my tall ambition? To comparison with those already lofty in pinnacle?

With a fabulous goal, mediocrity is distasteful. I'm cursed by an ideal—it binds me its slave. I salivate my whole starvation to a shrine of otherness from me.

I want that otherness to clasp me couplingly. I'm becoming fabulous. I'm being overtaken by what I didn't have. Soon, it's one with my me. The fabulous *is* me. Thus I'm sung, fulsomely, by my fans galore. Oh, they envy me, some do. I have it, they don't. Well, I'm it. I and the fabulous are a fit. Those devoid, do without. All those unfabulous outsiders. From within my fabulous, I look outside to them. They look *in*, to me. These two crucial viewpoints merge interdependently. I *am* my admirers; and they're me, by identification. It's a sympathetic bond. What a unity! I bless them, and they me.

It's *fabulous*, to be what I am. Odd, I wasn't *always* this way. I'm so *naturally* it. It's me, pure and through, true blue. I'm what the fabulous is, it's there, at me. I'm its home. It shines out *through* me. I'm its see-through vessel, its pure medium, the very vehicle to embody it. It's *mine*, now: or I'm its. Or it's a non-ownership of us both. I'm a borrowed suit, one of so many, worn by the indiscriminate fabulous—till it discards me. I'm but a rag, to keep the Fabulous warm. I'm its current style. I'm its God, on loan. The me that I am is now the home of the fabulous. I'm its local address—I'm being rented. It has a seat in me. For how long a stay? Or am I one inn, on its way?

GUESS WHO'S A CELEBRITY!

By a happy accident, I basked in celebrity's glory, by rumor's mistake. I was a stranger at a party. The other people there (including the hosts) didn't know me. I was an indirect guest, by some fluky chance. By the appearance I presented there, someone—I never found out who—started the rumor that I must be "So-and-So," whose name at the time was very much in the limelight of high oblique mystery-following that caught a huge segment of popularity appeal on the crest of the wave of a reputation.

But that mystery man I was confused for shunned direct photographic exposure, whether for television or for still photography. That left his face and his body too indeterminate to be determined; thus creating for me an opportunity to be mistaken for him, on the identity grounds of a flexible, plastic margin of how rumor had drawn his general picture which I was seen to fit into, by what I had in common with how the mystery original was generally by abstract populace consensus reputed to be believed to somehow look.

Thus I was pegged. Someone at the party was "certain." That sent a daisy chain wave link electrifyingly throughout the depth and breadth of the party, on the rousing wings of my "discoverer's" urgently whispered conviction, which indeed started the identity ball rolling: which swept me up bodily and facially into the very being himself of the mysterious celebrity I had suddenly been selected to personally be, to the full extent of my total being, down to what I *was* deep down in my soul, in the intimate essence of myself.

I played along, I didn't deny. Such gratuitous glory doesn't often fall into my plain lap. I'd be every inch the role of the glittering personage so generously assigned to me, on so sweeping and consummate a scale as to be the genuine article in purely mistaken identity.

I was being buttered up. Some stunning women were oozing their charms at me, in opportunity's beckoning. Such is the
public good fortune of a celebrity—which a celebrity might tire
of, but not the one whose brief fortune it was to impersonate
him.

("Brief"? "Impersonate"? Let me *always be* him. This was my
magic wish.)

To avail myself was only human. Why not settle down to enjoy the rare fruits of a mistake as fulsomely flattering as it was
excitingly unexpected?

All heads were turned toward me. Guests spoke to me, clusters surrounded me, some followed behind as I strolled into
the welcome center of a new cluster. I played to the hilt the big
glamor hit I had now smoothly melted into.

It went buzzing to my *own* head. My head was quite turned.
I believed more and more that I truly *was*—on the strength of
mob certitude and their fawning over me and falling over me—
the celebrity himself, done to a turn, from top to toe, in the embodied image of what he truly was, drawn to the finest detail
from the core of an entire self.

The circumstances made all too irresistible my proud assumption of the identity consigned to me by the overwhelming
party consensus amounting unanimously to a collective offering that put refusal out of the question, so concerted and "official" was the honor bestowed on me by edict and dignity of a
group act, the sanction thrust on the one by the many, a granted
esteem to be borne with becoming humility, in rich gratitude;
what was conferred on me, imparted to me, put me soaring
above the joint donors: to them I was bound, for the magnificently received eminence that I deigned, deliciously to accept.
"They" wanted me so. Bewildered, I was willing to lend my own
complete credulity to the transformation of my identity from
the previously unknown me (a stranger to the whole party, in-

cluding the hosts) to the new false me in the belief of which I co-operated in self-deception, to fall in with the illusion of the pack and to give myself "authentically" to the role wholeheartedly endorsed by the chosen actor of it, pulling the wool over his own eyes in company to the prevailing assumption that assumed terrifying proportions in the mass hysteria of a certainty pounced on publicly in their own discovered midsts.

How the women fawned on me! What a sumptuous array of choice I was plunged into! I could "have" anyone of them, that very night itself!

I had a pocket diary. I whipped it out, with a pen, and (surrounded as I was with celebrity admirers) quickly jotted down this on-the-spot, in-the-heat-of-the-fray entry of willful self-deception on self-reflection's self-perception:

"Here I am, the celebrity himself, at the crest of his roaring wave. The prevailing belief that I am he—with its hysterical content—spreads to my own head, and *I* take up the belief too, in the hypnotic frenzy of all his warm acclaim.

"Henceforth—till further notice at least—I *am* he. As I'm scribbling, I make a fascinating spectacle: a celebrity in a private jet.

"From so many angles, I'm the focal dot of the whole concentration of eyes.

"Where is the 'me' who came quite unannounced, anonymously to this party? That unheralded, pre-discovered stranger? Discarded? Lost in the shuffle? Laid aside? He vanished. He was me.

"Will I ever recover that guise I once had, prior to this recently acquired glamor? Is my transformation total, and permanent?

"No, my glamor is *not* recently acquired. In my heart I believe this: I was *always* that celebrity. Or rather, he has always been me, from birth's earliest conception, from the dawn of the womb of nativity's inception. I was even christened his name; and whatever befell him in all his life's experiences, are the sum of whatever happened to me—it's all been in *my* life.

"I wasn't born a celebrity; but in time's own ripe maturity I rose to such status by popular acclaim. What I've ever been and only been is that person himself, who only recently gained such prominence and celebrityhood in fickle fortune's favor in vogue's mystery code and fashion's wayward puzzle with the world.

"I'm being ogled. Time to put away this pocket diary and pen in their allotted interior pocket of my close-to-the-vest vest of my three-part suit.

"From a bevy of pretty women, I'll thrill one by choosing her my favorite. Then, graciously, I'll reply to a few more clamoring questions, before—with my selected queen in my arm—retiring from my idolaters, my fans, my already mushily melted mess of slain admirers. How strange the night has been—yet perfectly normal."

That ended the diary entry. I replaced diary and pen in the customary vest pocket.

Beaming, I return to my "public," phasing myself out of the party with some gracious replies, and my chosen beauty dangling on my arm.

I'm he from top to toe: every inch of the celebrity in question—no longer in question. He's myself, and retroactively has ever been so, even in his pre-celebrity days, before his humble status underwent ascension to the mystery crown of vast repute (though unseen in still photographs or by moving television camera). How grand I am, while taking my leave from the worshiping assemblage with, clinging or dangling from my famous arm, the thrilled pick-up chosen almost by chance in the whimsy of my grand privilege, being such a fabled character as I am, striding through the party rooms with

majestic aplomb, the nonchalance of the great, in casual magnificence, casting to the multitude (that gapes and gapes) my
democratic goodbye as though I were just one of them—an affectation of equality as a magnanimous gesture, a formal act of
sincere hypocrisy.

"To *your* place," I ordered my pickup. Her eyes were shut,
ecstatically to obey. A cab turned up, almost by command. We
floated in together, as by enchantment. She poured all over me
in a purr. Fame transforms everyone with whom it comes into
contact. But within the breast of those whom fame blesses, one
essentially remains unchanged, wearing only surface glory to
the magic tune of the world.

A MYSTERY FIGURE

The party was going full-blast. Whoopie was being made by the merrimentalities who tooted on horns or eked noise from whatever came to hand—or mouth. Guzzling was being done, with sloshing, from bottles and glasses that sparkled with the semi-danger of the dark-interior-contained intoxicants that lapped in tidal waves and danced to frothy currents and cross-flows, languidly wicked or gushingly stirred with whirling liquid menace.

One figure stood out, in abstaining and being abstemious, sternly still in the midst of all the blur and stir of commotion and motion.

He was a mystery figure. He was conspicuously a non-participant in the active bustle of social commingling pleasure and free feats of self-helpful open accessible indulgence under the permissive sway of the libertudinous mob under the common rule of approved forms of naughtiness sanctioned by the "everybody-doing-it" structure of group conformity in the lax policing of rules decorously broken by the consent of the malgoverned in ritual release from civilized constraints, within a tame pattern that restricts the freedom that so shockingly seems promoted, as though this were a game limited in choice and option, played by guests who jealously police, in convivial joviality, all the everyone-elses in tight surveillance despite the chaos popularly assumed with roaring voices and fierce drinking and stumble-steps.

The mystery figure was somber, sober, and of a different rhythm, in sole dissent from the genial celebrants of whatever occasioned by pretext or observance that rather rowdy party.

Who was he? What was he doing there? Had he been invited, or had he "crashed"? Why was, in countenance and expression, he so out of step, out of spirit, apart from, the prevailing tone of the general coherence?

He wasn't dressed like us. His hair, his everything-about-him, were non-observant of current styles and fashion's coercive but tolerantly accepted tyranny that blends pervasiveness over scattered souls.

He stood alone, speaking to no-one; nor did anyone care to approach him. He had a forbidding air, a stubbornly anti-social stance, and a seedy eccentricity that hinted of a bum or tramp dubiously decked out in a dressing-up that missed the mark through an incorrigible inexpertness that bespoke the "loner," the drifting, semi-autistic outsider who habitually failed to heed the signals that the rest of us alertly make a constant study of, to keep in the swim and central mix of approval's promiscuous web of graded mutuality loosely hinged together.

The stereotype of a "bum" is, of course: when a free-drink opportunity smilingly shows a benign heaven's favor, to avail himself, and to drink heavily, even to swill, before this magic offering is unexpectedly withdrawn, as a frowning curtain comes down to curtail the glorious wicked license that needed to be snatched up while the going and getting had been—mirage-seeming—there.

This mystery-figure must not have been a bum. He seemed oblivious of, untempted by, the unlimited access of drinks to suit any and every species of palate, thirst, or random grasp.

(Lots of money went into this party—hence the great full bar. Whether the funds were from private hospitality, or commercial budget in a promotional enterprise of an artistic or otherwise bent, is forgotten by your faithful scribe.)

Periodically, we all darted stares, in a mild puzzle of wonderment or an uneasy sting of curiosity, at that mystery figure who stood, solitary, so clearly apart from our dense close cordial mass of unexceptional merrymakers under the "riot" spell in full fledge as guests in consort—or concert: cells to one overall spirit or party-body, therefore subject to uniform regulatory policy.

I sought out the host or hostess, to inquire, "Who is that odd duck? He's disturbingly weird. How'd he get here?"

"Search me. *I* didn't invite him. But I only *live* here—so it's not my province."

"Were invitations sent by others, beside yourself?"

"This occasion was drummed up by a group of us as separate inviting agents. So it's hard to trace the precise source of any particular soul's happening to be here, due to the complex multiple-invitation-agency of the disunited ringleaders who weren't in concert as to which potential guests to let know by general word of mouth or express intentioned specified inviting. That mystery figure surrounded by a solitary air barrier of insulated incommunicableness, is *here*. I find him no danger or threat. So I'll let him be, instead of having him ejected. I'm too decent a person—aside from the incidental fact that I only *live* here—to ask an apparently harmless, somewhat eccentric-looking quiet mystery figure to leave. I pride myself not only on good manners but on goodness quite apart from manners. So let's have another drink, and go mingle and talk with people and forget or ignore the weird, unexplained presence of that odd bird."

"Good idea. But I have a mind to go up to him and talk to him."

"Is he an obsession?"

"Admittedly so. I'd like to get to the bottom of the little mystery element he's incongruously introduced to otherwise an invariably uniform gaiety of the jolly proceedings here."

"Well, you're welcome to query him; but don't persecute him with a harrying, harassing inquisition that violates the pride of his remaining so retiringly private and keeping his own counsel in spurning liberal opportunities to join in and share in our innocent frolics and noisy guzzling."

With that, the host or hostess, who lived there, merged in with the blaring party now in progress, now at its peak, now alcoholically at its prime group level of collectively averaged out inebriation consumption.

Hesitantly, but with the determination fortified by curiosity and much drink, I went up to the mystery figure. There I was, at eye level with him. I stood boldly in front of him, before him, addressing him face to face, but with a beseeching, inquiring glare or stare unsupported, as yet, by the impress of words.

I could see: he wasn't "there."

His eyes were inward-turned, as were whatever thoughts he was having. Though I'd "confronted" him like a challenge, he really didn't notice me. I might as well not have been there. I was absent to him. *He* looked absent, in vacancy. I could no more address or confront him than I could a post or other construction of inanimate nature, mineral material, or sense-devoid artifice.

No smell issued from him. He appeared bathed enough, though visibly his attire was negligent. And he had recently shaved.

I retreated. I got involved in conversations—one thing led to another, in gregarious interchanges from group to group of people caught up in the hectic uproar of high decibel shouting and loud accelerations of drink's uncensored remarks.

Later, I returned to the mystery figure. He wasn't there—or anywhere. I asked people where he was—no-one had seen him vanish, though everyone had been glancing uneasily at him earlier when his conspicuousness most exerted itself on thresholds of casual consciousness during otherwise a standard "wild" party: a big bash, that didn't depart too noticeably from customary modes of normality, as though almost supervised by dull sticklers of reactionary tradition finely finished with every familiarity.

I looked around—he was nowhere.

The *party* turned out to be forgettable, being too "typical" of its kind. Not, however, that haunting figure. It's long years afterwards. I still find myself dwelling on him. He was that party's main "production," as an enduring episode, in recurrent memory. He's the surviving relic—all that remains of that conventional bedlam.

Where is he—if anywhere? Where had he come from, where did he then go?

He's gone. I know I'll never meet him in that "recognizable" form. He's scattered, like nature's elements in mortality's finite brushing with vanishing glimpses met in the apparitions of phantoms and then encountered never solidly again but only in shady recesses of minds like mine that accelerate to their eventual decomposing with such rapidity that I'm scared—I long for that mystery figure. I was warmly much younger then, crowded close with fellow yellers over the brash din we were all creating. I was part of the swarm. The mystery figure was another sort of me. He completed the puzzle.

A TRIAL OF SILENCE

The other guests could see, too plainly, how I wasn't fitting in. Everybody else seemed to be talking to someone else. All but me. I was stuck in a rut of verging just on the outside of the border-boundary-barrier between those who were talking with someone (all but me) and the one whose obvious lonely misery showed all too tellingly that he was the only one all by himself, unable to catch on, to hook on, to any one of the quite-a-few conversational couples or clusters: whose circles of talk seemed openly accessible to other joiners-in come over from other conversational pairs or groups in graceful currents of shift, but were mystically closed (expressly, it seemed) to me alone; so that even an *attempt* on my part to get into a word exchange with anyone at all seemed foredoomed into a dreamlike foolhardiness of futility in a methodical torpor of slow, cumbersome non-motion.

Not that there was a *conspiracy* to exclude me. I looked so abjectly *willing*—so despairingly eager—to engage anyone in a talking ritual (whether my role was first to listen, or to speak): that my *Need* was brandished like a leper's stigma, a quarantine signpost warning away all those too healthy to wish to trade in their wholesome routes of health for the morbid curse of my contamination.

How hangdog, abject, hopeless, and forlorn did I appear: and my Appearance was obviously all too truthfully replete with the full laden content of the very substance of Being. Directly proclaimed in the appearing, the state of my being was clear to all. I was to be avoided, just perversely because being avoided was precisely what I was trying to escape. An unwritten law united the other party guests in keeping me unspoken to, in letting me squirm and languish in an acutely uncomfortable, sorely anguished, deeply humiliating, brutally embarrassing position of feeling *left out*.

The explanation for my *feeling* left out lay in my actually *being* left out. My feeling was no lie. It truthfully fed on what fully *was*.

Shunned, ostracized, avoided, cut, ignored in a way of being deliberately neglected—odd man out, I was. The crowd—that big conforming bully— sensed I was stung and hurt in the bitter sentence of an exclusion from the central warmth of its inside self. Its unspoken joint unified purpose that the crowd concertedly manifested in ruthless mechanism of its totality in faithful coherence by each organ member under complete direction from the sum of the bulk they comprised, was to let me stew, to leave me be, to sustain the poignant notoriety within the party confines of my pained isolation: which stood out in the frenzied bruise of a blush, a sullen oneness I labored in vain to hide.

Should anyone break ranks to come forward to succor me and redress my distress by addressing me and impressing an undepressing fellow-feeling on my bereft state of conspicuous solitude, thus letting me join in and link beings with him or her in the warmth and quickening of an exchange to break the icicle encasement of my frozen mouth, ice-clogged ears, and cold-encased, heart-hardened social breast:—that would-be humanitarian would himself risk the detestation and disfavor of the disapproving group from whose ranks he broke faith in his weak violation of their closed front that must maintain me as an untouchable and unspoken-to, gloomed in a continual "silent treatment" to keep me ever at arms-length the unwilling, pleading, straining, enforced, inwardly protesting, outwardly hypocritically stoical, outsider: an outsider inside what was—for all the rest—a pleasant, fully-mixing party, easy in the warmth of gay drifts of talk, convivial encounters presided over by the merriment of drink—altogether, a hearty affair.

Yet, unparanoiacally speaking, there was never a "conspiracy" afoot. It just turned out to *seem* like there was. Most of the guests hadn't known the rest of the guests, so there was no collusion, no premeditated common front designed for shutting me out in one master plot that planned to undermine my well-being on an occasion when everyone else's well-being was well provided for by the prevalent harmony that stamped the party—by all accounts save mine— strictly an unmitigated success, by standards bearing an ultimate banner of the ideal absolute to be hoped for from any party, rarely attained, thereby demonstrating the great pure rarity of this party's standing in the graded ranks of a true ideal.

The against-me-ness of the group as a uniform effort or stand or stance, was a spontaneous thing drawn from the pressure and impulse of the moment, to exploit the seized-upon occasion of my looking crestfallen and woebegotten. Given the opportunity to perpetuate the much-noted spectacle of my obvious-to-all weakness (all too glaring to everyone separately in the loosely disjointed assemblage that was the party), the guests smelled a wounded animal in their midst. In mob cruelty, in group sadism, these separate people, without "banding together," finding me at their mercy dying to be spoken to, acknowledged, accepted, taken in—they concurrently and unanimously all joined in, so to speak, in ganging up on the outsider to bar his entry once his entry was already seen as increasingly difficult; since timidity and shyness grew insurmountable in me as the situation ever worsened with the conspicuous apparentness of my palpable exclusion in a mounting fit or torment, with excruciating discomfiture and the wild, burning vaudeville on the improvised stage of my unease.

There was no prior policy to program my torture. But once my grueling ordeal had become nicely evident, everyone held back in a loathing to grant me such rescue and relief as I all too readily craved. I was everyone's popular cause, to "let be." Strictly not to be interfered with, in the private agony of a passively publicly permitted crucifixion quite fascinating to witness in their passive participation in their spectator sport, tossing me psychically into the lion-infested arena, as the hungry beasts stood by to watch me devour myself impaled helpless on the unpopularity cross, left to be in deliberate bestiality, as I ate my lonely heart out in sardonic view of all.

Should I leave? It was too late to break the spell. My lot was cast, my effect made. I'd have to give up, and flee.

But no. It looked like a promising party. I'd come from quite a distance, with elaborate transport changes, just to get there.

And there I was. So why quit? I'd brazen it out, see it through, and stick to my guns. I'd break in and be spoken with, once I'd drunk enough to make penetrating thrust and edge past the crucial barrier of the word spoken and responded to. I'd hold out. I was held fast, paralyzed. No use bluffing. I was the silent prey, the hunter's game, stalked by being held off and pointedly ignored as I trembled precariously on the brittle brink of solitude's fragile, stern pride: badly needing and yet not daring to break down in a sobbing plea for the gentle attention of someone else's voice caressing the barren dirge of my soul moaning its remaining so sole, letting out the great grief of an interior wail unheard by these stony, tacitly mocking, sporting, unrelenting, firm, smug, bully-cowardly onlookers, who delighted in the odor of a stricken, panic-close, near-down member of their gloating species, prattling away so easily to each other, squandering floods of words any few of which, if addressed to *me*, would redeem me from my fallen grace and save my whole socially sunken soul.

So I drank and drank, to shoot my courage up to the starting point of somehow bursting through and initiating, at my own instigation, an iceberg-shattering excursion into the realm of conversation—banal though it may be, in common carving of the trite phrase uniting people by the dull thread of words.

Drinking, drinking—still I was stultified, stuck sober cold in my block of self from which my emergence was held ever back in bitter paralysis and the grim, dried tears of despair drawn clenched in the exquisite spasm-bound constraint of effort-dead futility.

The party got gayer, everyone was happy. If only the whole world, outside, could prove to be for those people, ever and always, what the party had become tonight.

Why should I begrudge everyone else their happiness, just because it was barred to me alone? Their cruelty to me didn't exempt them from deserving their party happiness tonight. So I was their slight sacrificial victim? I'd willingly pay that price, for such a rare and fine party.

Their delight, not mine. But by proxy, mine. I belonged, too. The unspoken-to, the pointedly excluded, the roundly rejected—I had my part, my place. So I played it, willingly, once I was drunk enough not to resent it.

You happy people! You dear, darling bunch! My intimate, distanced tormentors-by-neglect! We're in a grand party together. I play my minority part, my sole unique role. I'm a discordant note. But the note is joined to the score. It's one drunken music, together.

My note? The negative one, of silence swallowed with all the drink I had. Silence, surrounded by *their* noisy gaiety: the silent, scorned, observed, and kept center of the happy din of such a sweet party—for them.

Then what? The rest got lost, in drink's blur. My memory doesn't last out the party I had to take mental leave of, to endure.

There they were, those others, joined. In their brimming clusters. Those jovial, at-home guests.

Thereafter, I'm a blank. I recollect nothing. Drunken oblivion blotted out the party's end. My enforced silence *may* have been broken. I've seen no-one to ask, of that party, since that time.

The party hasn't continued into my present life. I lead a social, gregarious life, involved with other people's lives, amid much talk, back and forth. But at the party, I knew, and remained knowing, no-one. They're fading, those brutal excluders. They're dimming, from the finite arc of my life's huge party-span, that plows through years and people and slowly recedes from the ever-distancing pole of that crucial organic event, my birth.

CATHERINE WON QUICKLY, LOST SOON AFTER

What a beautiful girl! All my life up till then had gone by, and I had had no idea that she even existed!

(In my first ten years of life I couldn't have been blamed for not knowing of her existence, for all that time she still had never been born.)

I was early at a party, so was she, we were the first to have arrived; the only other person there being our hostess (who never had to take the trouble to arrive for she lived there).

The hostess said "Here's Catherine," then *completed* the introduction by telling Catherine *my* name. So we stood formally introduced, which ruled out any possibility of my accosting her and "picking her up" in that wild state of our being unmet. That would have been romantically daring, but it was too late. Our relationship started on a harmless footing of civilized domesticity. I wanted to re-unestablish it into a wild, uncontrollable adventure. That would introduce a basis for impetuous passion that would sweep us into the ravages of bondage; and give life a rawness, which would admit of only the most poignant love and resist any other cultivation whatever.

But first I had to win her heart, to make her *want* to touch deepest instincts with me (including, ideally, sex).

I foresaw an obstacle to our union: a girl that beautiful would naturally already have a "boy-friend," her heart would have a prior engagement, a deep committing involvement that would preclude the superfluous extension into a new entanglement. This was my legitimate fear, for how could anyone that beautiful be not already "taken up," since thousands of men must have competed for so fair a one's favors, and of all those candidate suitors surely one must have been foremost and pleased her passing fair in love and fancy. And such a one couldn't have been such a fool as to forego the foreverness upon such a winning, for she was exceeding worth keeping, however fastidiously jaded her fickle captor would be.

So I came upon her too late. But where was her dream beau? Why was Catherine unescorted, and an early arriver at that? My hope flew up. She wasn't paired! Oh then, here I step in, to announce I'm enchanted. Should she care, I mean to grab her, right there, and relinquish her only when death pries open my arms of amorous holding. I'll clamp her in a grip so smotheringly fierce we'll be fastened. For so I feel, which she must confirm to close our mated cause and settle truth upon so far an ideal. Catherine's looking. I pour down blazing speech:

"I love you. Be mine."

"But we've only just met."

"No matter. I feel as though I've known you all my life."

"But you're so sudden."

"Love can't delay, for it had always dreamed upon the object that now confirms it."

"*Me*? How *dare* you refer to me as an object! You're impertinent, impudent, possessive, but nice, as well. I like you, but don't love you yet."

"Hurry, please. I need you reciprocal in order to master you with the upper hand."

"Unhand me, you cur! What are your intentions?, that I may not know you for an imposter."

"Honorable. I propose marriage."

"When?"

"Now, if not sooner."

"But the party's only just started! Don't spoil the fun."

"Solemnity, not—as you put it—'fun,' is the earnest of my love's devotion. Frivolity would be out of place, now."

"Oh, you're so bourgeois. Go lighter with your suit, or 'tis like I'm by a cleric woo'd, whose God's wrath would unsmile him most frowningly."

"Look, Catherine, love is serious business. Its aim is that you may bear children to pilot the world to its fate."

"Oh, your Victorian pomposity!"

"Mock me not, fair wench!"

"Nay, nay, I'm hard press'd. You count my every laboring breath, while I cry out, 'Air, air!' "

"I would win thee, wooingly."

"And I'd be won, by nought but thou, sweet fair."

"Then nuptial troth is ours to plight?"

"Sure. But not tonight."

"When, when? I can't wait!"

"But only now the guests are beginning to arrive."

"Then now's the time to leave. Who wants a party, when we have each other, no addition to which is needed, or even desirable, for it would spoil our maximum minimum."

"But a party *caused* us to meet. Don't we *owe* it to the party to stay?"

"The party did its purpose, by us, at least. Its end thus achieved, it's all useless dregs, so let's leave."

"I won't!"

"Then I'll stay. I can't leave without you."

"You'd *better* not. An argument already!, at the start! What will our *later* life be like?"

There *was* no later life, As more guests arrived, men kept going over to Catherine, and gradually cut her off from me, She must have promised her hand to most who asked. She left the party with the last man to arrive. In retrospect, had I arrived too early? She had proven fickle, so in retrospect was I not well spared of her? Catherine, quick and easy, and early to lose. I was the same, but different, from before the party.

MEL IS CONSTANTLY MISSING SOMETHING. HE'S LEFT OUT OF MORE THAN HE MANAGES TO TAKE IN. POOR MEL, SO FINITE

There's a big party on, everybody is talking, animated discussions, interesting things being said, especially in group A. Just at the height of this interestingness, Mel's bladder *insists* that all of Mel go to the bathroom. "Why can't you go yourself?" Mel asks, but the bladder replies, "Discharging urine requires your assistance." So off goes the whole and the part, together, of Mel: like a very pregnant woman, and the fetus she's bulging with.

After this private act, Mel hurries back to his spot in group A, where the talk is waxing with intense merriment and sparkling rejoinders, squeezing entertaining information out of a subtle blend of subjects.

Mel speaks up: "I went to the bathroom but now I'm back. What did I miss?"

"How long were you away?"

"Seven or eight minutes, if you go by the clock."

"As the clock goes, so go I."

"Who said what, in my absence?"

"We said plenty, but within context. What was said depended on all the rushing continuity of accumulation built steadily up. If you were left out at that phase, accept your bad luck. We can't recapitulate. It's too complex."

"I feel left out."

"Did you *have* to go to the bathroom?"

"My bladder *insisted*: I had no choice."

"A most untimely insistence."

"Please fill me in. All you people were so gaily talking, as I reluctantly took my leave; and on my return, you were even *more* enthusiastically communicating. What had transpired, in the mean time, during all that?"

"You've just disrupted our flow. You've stifled our spontaneity, and have imposed a self-conscious pall on the wild fun of our impromptu proceedings in the verbal bash-the-ball-about. I hardly recall, now. You've put a stop to it."

"You about murdered," another non-Mel said, "the heart and soul of our lively chat. Why couldn't you just *accept* having been voluntarily left out? Instead, all furtherance is lost, for us, the group A communicants."

"I'm *always* left out," said Mel sadly; "or nearly so. I was left out all the years of my life before I was born. Think of what I missed everywhere from all the social gatherings the world over. I just wasn't there, at the time."

"Even had you been alive every year since the advent of Man to the triumph of Evolution, you couldn't have attended the frequent simultaneity, the constant ubiquity, of human talk everywhere. Even with the fastest airplane ready at immediate service. So of *course* you missed out on more that went conversationally on than what you were able to take in by being present at. Alertness is only sporadically local to where at a given time you are. You lost human history before you, mainly by simply not being there. But here you are, back from the bathroom, participating in our transient Group A, which is now dissolving. You preside at its liquidation, which you've contributed to. We're breaking up. Let our segments join the other groups still undisbanded, that have informally formed within the overall chaotic plurality of this multiply talkative party. Henceforth, we're scattered entities. Group A has faded away, as local recent legendary history. Long live Group A: It's dead, now."

Thus, Mel got lost, in other units. The party crowded off into shifting groups. Mel took in what he could, while the hour grew late. His experience was finite. He didn't have unlimited access. By being in one partial group, he missed what other groups in other corners were wagging on about. He was missing more than he was getting: always falling behind: at this rate, never to catch up. Nor could he blame it on the bladder. He was only one person. Lost, in trifling pockets of humanity's teeming vastness sprawling into numerous numericalities. What could Mel do? Time and space and abundance beat him. His share, so tiny. He'd throw it back, having lost All.

A CONSTANTLY LONELY VARIETY

My incessant loneliness. Loneliness feeds on itself. It finds ways and means. It hunts out parties. It gluts itself with people. It devours social occasions. It bloats itself on innumerable conversations. Endless telephoning, rounds and rounds of visits, plans of meetings and introductions, all the periodical keeping up. Arranging get-togethers. Happy boredom with friends and acquaintances, the nervous tedium of the social rounds. Gregarious anxiety, you can never have enough of it. Contacts get contacted. Hello and goodby, and the last goodby is the first farewell. The diversified repetition, for the lonely palette.

PERSUADED FROM LONELINESS TO COMPANY

I live at a remove.

Why not join in?

Then the "me" would be sacrificed to what I join; and where would *I* be?

You'd be *part* of things.

(Contemptuously:) Part!? How paltry! I would preserve my whole being, remote from what would dissolve it by an incorporation in a bigger, unwieldy thing. *(Mimes appropriately to following:)* I'm tidy as I am, neat in a compact package. Why not *keep* me that way? Crowds of people diffuse the personality. Why should my defined edges rub off in the multiple promiscuity of friction? My boundaries should be inviolate, trim and kept up: like a garden plot, hedged in to private plan and possessive purpose.

So you keep apart?

Groups couldn't claim me: I'm firmly solitary.

Are you far from *love*'s contact?

Passion's beam dims and cools down by the time it reaches me.

Does the hearthhold of a family bosom warm your participation?

My connections have long been severed, and I'm free, relative-ly.

Are you any organization member?

Not. I'm only me.

But what of *friendship*'s golden circle? Do you meet cronies at a party and celebrate?

But I come only single, and leave singly, too.

Are you standoffish, with them?

Drink carouses me into a hearty mood.

So you're *socially* human, at times?

Yes, a dizzy fellowship makes comrades dear, illusionary buddies, for a while. The bond bulges out, but soon snaps. Then I'm restored to my angry solitude, as before.

But why should anger enter it?

Pride was hurt, that I thought of puncturing solitude ever, in some shared occasion of frivolity, when drink unpaints things as they are and looms the petty bubble of a myth. Which reality is delighted to prick, and back I fall, surly with contempt, and all lies flat and desolate that I dared attempt away from it. Better to *accept* than regret later.

How dear are people to you, when malevolence holds you to such gloom at failing them! Succeed to a belonging friend, is the therapy I would cling to, for your bright prospects. For privacy is a moaning of life away. How this eager we would be, for some strokes of popularity! How much misery this would ease, in the sordid cell of loneliness! Be warmly melted to some social liberation. Clutch another, different and alike. The requited aura of generosity is the double knowing of the same heart. Joys inaccessible to the hermit! Remove your steeled ice layers against it, and be moved in others' directions. The current will once more flow, and the linked man is more the man, tapped open to his fellows nearby. Responsive, with open numbers of lives to be the greater for. And share a woman's world as well. Such dormant faculties urge to go out! Be kept by, and the keeper of, the manifold versions of your own contrast. And earn your identity in the hands of others. The demands are full, that life is in the midst of people, enriching the deep nerves of the individual man, nourished by the outward contact, esteemed in the clash; then, when repairing inward, being more for it: retreating with honor, and the throngs of experience that vibrate to the inner being. And serve solitude by peopling it. Let the echoing voice ring down that chamber. Belonging is to mankind, or the self's choice of samples. A girl friend close to you, or your married wife; and men reliable, for the wager of discussion. Friends define what person you are, and *you*'re molding *them* at the same time. This *must* be good. From tribe to neighbor to familiar, the contact closes in: and we well out.

Then will you show me how?

I'll guide you, as friendship's personal escort. Be shown.

I'll go. I trust you. Lead me.

And so you're now more than you started. For you're me, as well.

A welcome addition. It rounds me be*yond* myself. Before, I hoarded: nothing. Now, I have all to give.

THE HUGE STARVATION APPETITE THAT LONELINESS DIETS ON

Come to my party.

(Elated:) Joy!

Why "joy"?

By holding a party, you're cutting off my loneliness at its source.

What *is* its source?

Scarcity of people.

(Incredulously:) What!? With the population explosion these days!? And the birth rate booming!?

(Pathetically:) I just want a friend.

Oh, how pathetically unselective you are! Haven't you taken lessons in improving your popularity?

I don't have the skill to be popular, and it can't be developed.

How defeatist! Well, I'm glad to be cutting off your loneliness at its source.

Yes, better than cutting off my *meat* from its *sauce.*

Of course. Do you like to eat savory food?

Of course. How many courses?

Don't be coarse. Well, I invite you: Have lunch with me.

As your guest?

Yes, I'll pay.

Good. But won't my company bore you?

We can make table conversation.

Fine. We'll dish up the talk. Let's go.

(Pause. Later:)

What a great meal that was!

Yes, but you were a poor conversationalist.

My mind was on the food.

Oh. Your tongue would have been sufficient.

(Pause. Later:)

Are you still with me! ? Go home!

Why do you want to shake me off?

You bore me! Leave me now. I want to be alone. Then come to my party tonight.

(Elated:) Joy!

Why "joy"?

The party solves my loneliness problems.

(Skeptically scornful:) With *your* unpopularity? It'll only *compound* them!

Oh, then I won't go.

Why not?

One loneliness is enough; why make it multiple?

You're right. Then don't come.

Oh woe.

You *do* suffer, don't you?

I do. I depend on people. They're the only loneliness-curers I know.

Yes; but you don't *know* them.

I know; Oh woe.

Then come to my party tonight.

(Subdued elation:) Joy!

But why joy?

All those people! My loneliness can squeeze in between them, and get lost.

You expect them to crowd out your loneliness?

I do. With their rubbing friction.

Then your loneliness would be *sexually* stimulated.

Is that *bad*?

Think of the *promiscuity* involved.

Oh.

Come anyway. *(Making a move to depart:)* See you tonight.

Are you *sure* you're inviting me?

Of course. Your unpopularity will be challenged by the party, and squeezed out in the crush. Numerically, it'll be outnumbered.

That's helpful. It's so vast, itself.

What is?

This unpopularity I have. You know how vast it is? and the scope of its cosmic dimensions?

I don't even *hope* to know: It must be of *global* proportions!

It is!

And my party is only a minute speck!

Your speculation is correct.

(Awed:) What a loneliness you have!

Yes. It'll *nibble* at your party. But won't have a *full meal*.

HOW TO SUBSTITUTE FAILURE FOR SUCCESS AS A GOAL, SO THAT YOU'LL BE ABLE TO HAVE A GOAL THAT YOU CAN ATTAIN, AND FEEL A MASTERFUL POWER OVER WILL, BY AT LEAST "CONTROLLING" THE SITUATION, RATHER THAN STRIVING IN VAIN. FAILURE WILL "SEEM" LIKE SUCCESS, WHEN YOU ACTIVELY SOUGHT IT OUT. THEN YOU'LL HAVE SOME AUTHORSHIP IN IMPROVISING THAT FATE OF YOURS THAT HAD BEEN CREATED BY CIRCUMSTANCE BEYOND YOUR PERMISSION. THE ILLUSION WILL BE THAT YOUR OWN HANDS ARE ON THE WHEEL, IN PILOTING YOUR DESTINY. TAKEN FOR A RIDE, THE DRIVEN DRIVER SEEMS TO PRESIDE. THE FAILURE ROAD IS BY HIS OWN CHOICE, HE SEEMS TO DECIDE.

I arrived at a party at its very early and awkward stage, when there were as yet only the first few guests there, stone-sober and embarrassingly self-conscious. Painfully deliberate introductions only aggravated the lack of ease, which spread from each person to everyone else, in a painful contagion of martyrdom to arriving early.

The solution was to wait with patience till more and more guests should arrive to flood the room with the anonymous ease that would swallow up starkly individual stiffness.

There was also a more *im*patient method of dealing with the present awkward state: to swill down quantities of hard alcohol to blur the brain centers and unnerve the nerves of themselves.

That's what *I* especially did. It gave me a momentarily dizzy happiness. Not trusting the permanence of that, or its naturalness, I had to compound my inebriation by swallowing lots more down.

Thus artificial measure leads to heavier artifice, and nature is distrusted altogether.

Also, I hadn't eaten, that day; and this sudden onrush of drink made wild and merry in the void of my empty stomach: like children going on a wild rampage in a large house when the parents are away for a while and there's no adult present to act as a check.

The drink was going crazy in me. I was soon unaware that I was even at a party. By then, the party itself had a lively atmosphere, an easy-going gregaiety because of each guest's group immunity in a large and swarming crowd that overflowed the restrictions of conscience.

I was in a state of hazy oblivion. I went from one conversation to another in galloping stages of participation, taking a normal riot in my stride.

Then it occurred to me in a lucid interval with a flash of brief sobriety that I was a man womanless for months and that my secret intent goal in coming to this party was to pick up a woman and begin a love affair.

I gathered my mental resources together, to overcome the early drunkenness. I had to be clear-headed to stalk the available female prey; and with will-power I snapped loose from being muddle-headed. I cut out the drinking and concentrated on nourishing food, as well as availing myself of the considerate offer of warm coffee by my compassionate hostess (whoever she was).

So I "came to"; and resumed being inhibited.

Shyly, yet boldly, I engaged some pretty girls in chat, successively. But each time I conveyed amorous intentions I was informed that the girl was escorted and "going with someone"— a declaration of her inaccessibility, to halt my feebly enlarging overtures and cut down my gait of progress before its swirling tide could pick up momentum.

With my momentarily dashed but recovering ardor for the chase and the hunt, I would move over to approach the next prospect: who, in turn, would deal me the same message. I was now being generously discouraged.

Still cheerfully undaunted, I'd try again; even expecting to be rejected. I went on my fruitless pursuit. The girls were all "taken up." They had a steady boy-friend or a husband or a fiancé or were living with a fellow or had a love entanglement in some way. That cut me out into the cold. Pursuing in vain the girls I tried for, I was myself pursued by the grotesque phantom of a huge loneliness. This weighed down my heart, in hurt pride and bitter depression. In this cruel process, I could only persist.

Disappointment fed on itself, and that was what I looked for; it was easier to find, than its opposite, so it perversely granted me a goal *successful* of attainment, however initially and ultimately undesirable the success in that goal was, in going against my best interests on the whole, the advantage of finding a nice girl to love and be loved by. So I played my despair into a game, which somehow eased my desperation.

I was plunged in total loneliness, in the middle of the crowd. All the girls were "taken up." So then I started my second phase of drinking, that night: Not euphoria, but stupor, would await me.

This methodical misery-confirming, drop by drop, bloated me in a dungeon of foul black liquid, a pool for sordid drowning. The nadir of the evening was in its negative depth.

With my alert but soon crushed awareness that remained, I noticed that some new guests had arrived late. One of them was the girl of my dreams, encountered on the planet for the first time. I would ask for her hand in marriage, at the first opportunity.

She had entered alone: no man nearby. I had to act swiftly, before the swarms of my womanless competitors could get to her and start hurling words. (The party had a proportion of five

men to every two women, according to a professionally mathe-
matic statistician who was in attendance.)

I quickly blocked this dream girl's path and started wooing
her at once. She tried to move away, but that defensive impulse
or flight reflex proved to be arrested by a solid wall of people
with no hole for getting through. So she had to hold her ground,
while I raved on.

I was not making progress, in warming her heart. I vowed
my eternal love, but she seemed unmoved.

"Why so heartless?" I inquired.

"Your attack was too forward and sudden like a bolt," she
explained, "and rude, at that. It didn't leave me any room for
feeling out my own inner guidance in this matter. No sooner
I enter the party, when you're rushing down my throat, mad,
lonely, depraved. You're so lonely I can do nothing for it. Your
loneliness is chillingly cosmic. No single woman could cure it,
or mere mortal soul. I'm no nurse to minister to agony and distress. I want a man who's already calm and comfortable and
fortified happily with a woman. Then he wouldn't be so depen-
dent on me, for he'd have someone to fall back on. You, on the
contrary, are too imposing a responsibility for me. You'd be too
possessive and jealous, for in losing me you'd lose all your balance and sanity in a terrifying abyss. I can't make up for what
you lack, it's too awful a burden. So I'll let myself be seduced
tonight by a relaxed married man. It will be light, and easy to
digest."

Her speech, surprisingly articulate for so beautiful a
woman (as my poisoned logic would have it), was not designed
to instil confidence in me, or inflate my hopes with happy
prospects. It cornered me into uncontrollable sadness.

While I was savoring that worst of all lonely states, she
made her escape through a gap in the wall of people. I could

see her dimly at the opposite end of the room. Three men had all pounced on her, verbally. She was a popular magnet.

Her attraction continued as I tried to draw closer through the people. I would renew my thrust, and make failure another attempt. I'd be repulsed, and so win to the perverse goal, by losing out. The game was: to succeed in failure. That gave me control over the situation. I was no longer helpless, I knew what I wanted: rejection, complete and devastating. I'd force it from her again. The party was not in vain. It was fun, now that I opposed my own hope, and *sought out* the worst. Seeking it out made it seem not so bad. I was exercising choice; since my first choice was futile, and now this was the consolation to remain.

I aggressively pushed my way through. The dream girl was in an embrace, with a married man. I thrust myself between them, to upset their brief bliss, like an unwelcome wedge to pry apart parts that longed to cling.

The man would assert his masculinity, so he started to hit me, to prove what a man he was to the dream girl. I was soon on the floor. I had willed it all. I had asked for it. I was the master. My will was creating a scene. I had *some* effect, on reality, yet.

LARRY FIGHTS TO UNLONELY HIMSELF

Lonely Larry needed a girl for a long time. After having in earlier youth a succession of sweet and sour love affairs, he was now going through a stage of life, in his early middle-age, of incompatibility with all of the numerous girls he would meet in the desperate round of parties he'd go to, a continual bout of social gatherings he'd attend in his lonely hunt.

He felt himself, after "nothing happened" with every girl he collided with in a temporary state of psychological uncompoundability—he couldn't "connect" with any girl anywhere: it was like a disease. He romantically put himself in the shade as a "tragic figure," and nursed his bitter solitude with a sort of heroic self-pity. He felt like Lord Byron, only in reverse—without the conquests. His sexual deprivation acutely reinforced his emotional one. He was love-starved. He lived all alone.

He had a job by day, and in his spare time worked on history and biography, compiling notes toward being an author in those broad categories. He was a "man of letters"—as yet unpublished. He hoped to publish a book soon, to give him glory and status that would attract beautiful women who admire actual authors. He secretly hoped to be worshiped—adored as well. He was prepared, in turn, to worship and adore. He wanted *the* grand passion. But the world was cynical, and his city had slick codes of behavior for trendy-minded people on a lower key than his romantic aspirations. He wasn't of his time and place. He needed an extraordinary, timeless, placeless woman, *the* woman, transcending everything topical, nobly elevated above contemptible contemporary fashion. Larry was asking a lot—everything in fact. But he'd *give* everything as well. It would be an all-or-nothing thing, titanically scaled. It would be possessive, not casual. The sort of thing that Verdi knew about. The eternal.

Nothing less would do. Therefore, Larry conducted a fruitless search.

Frustrations piled up. Years of parties and gatherings and social events gave him nothing but romantic abortions, the miscarriages of sentiment. His loneliness got hardened. It shrinked-in its horizons. It lost the courage to hope. Its expectations withered. Despair had set in.

Despair, having succeeded desperation. Desperation had been frenzy, attempt after attempt. Despair was immobile. It was the giving up.

That was the state Larry was in, when he got himself invited (indirectly, for he never knew the host) to still another party. He was sick of parties, their disappointment. The end of a party had the same inevitable disaster, having made a corpse of each particular hope in the shape of any girl met there. The girls were indifferent, or escorted, or spoken for, taken up, engaged, married, involved, not interested. It was sickening.

Larry went to this one. He had been depressed for six solid months. A historical biography was due to be published in a year, but he was unknown, with no glamour of status about him. And he was unappealing to women, due to the smell of "failure" he unavoidably gave off—failure with women. He had the mark of the rejected, about him.

He drank and pursued, but no girl responded. The cruel pattern was repeating itself.

Now the party was thinning out, it was late after midnight, Larry was disconsolate, drunk, miserable. He felt acutely sorry for himself, through a vague and slobbering melancholy, and drink's euphoric diffusion of the soul's unbearables—enabling him to "put up" with them, like the veteran professional of suffering he now knew himself to be. Then, his "saviour" walked in.

She came with another girl, from whom she became detached in desultory wanderings through the remnants of that dying party. Brazen, Larry accosted her, with that false heartiness of hours of drinking. They found themselves chatting, Janet and Larry. And this Janet—special, a rarity. The dream of all time. A girl with a soul.

They just sat on the floor, side by side, holding hands intimately. They'd alternately gaze into each other's eyes, and shyly avert their eyes from each other. There was one current running through both, and the bond came natural. They were talking and talking, all this while. The talk was not surface skitter, not civil, not social, not polite: it "cut through" to their intimate cores, back and forth, like total depth surgery of familiar gentleness. It was natural, it seemed as if this had all been happening before, or should have been. There was so much to make up for now, for the sin of their never having met years before. They "knew" each other, immediately. It was pure recognition, turned revelation, and back to recognition. It wasn't even new. This had been going on for ages. But not till now had accident blessed it with confirmation.

The accident of this miracle meeting. The birth of very old love. Ripeness, toward which the unknown in mystery had unknowingly been approaching, in years of sad solitude. Larry loved her. He was redeemed.

He walked her home, invited himself in. She said no at the door. He knew by this that something was imperfect.

"Do you live with a man?"

"No, I'm alone, but I'm involved. I'd love you to be my friend."

"No, this is love, not friendship. Get rid of the other man. I want you for myself."

"Don't be so possessive. You act like you've owned me all your life. I feel threatened and devoured by you. What's happened tonight was too rare and good to be true. Let's back down to earth. You can't abduct me to the skies—my wings are occasional, not regular. I want to return to my own life, where you can't dictate terms as a tyrant by love. Take out a paper and write down my phone number. Let me hear from you, but not too soon."

And so Larry moped home. He hadn't even kissed Janet at her door. Their parting put a theatrical anticlimax upon the evening. Larry was severely let down. He plunged into a love gloom. This turned into exhilaration by the time he reached his own home. Confidence buoyed him. He would win her. This time, it was the "real thing."

He phoned her urgently, frequently, incessantly, till finally she had her number changed and made it private, unlisted. This shut Larry off, and he gave up. Now he never tries. His hope is dead, but officially he has longer to live yet. He'll age in a squalid loneliness. Stale unrelieved solitude. His book was published, and went unnoticed.

BROWN FINDS A GIRL AT CLOSE QUARTERS IN A
PARTY PACKED CROWDED TOGETHER SO TIGHT
THAT MEMORY IS LOOSE AND LETS THAT FLIMSY
ENCOUNTER SLIP AWAY FROM THAT SUMMED BODY
OF EXPERIENCE, THE GIRL REMAINING UNDES-
IGNATED TO THE SOULFUL OF HER SPECIFICS;
THOUGH BROWN SOUGHT HER IN A GENERAL WAY
IN THE MIST OF DISPERSAL ONCE THE PARTY FELL
APART TO SET SEPARATION AT LIBERTY AND UNCOU-
PLE THE PROMISCUOUS COINCIDENTS RUBBED OFF
IN HEATFUL EXCHANGES IN COLLISIONS OF AIM-
LESS LUST FIXATED IN THE BREVITY OF ROMAN-
TIC ILLUSIONS ON PARTNERS TEMPORARILY COME
UPON ON SUCH CHANGE COMBINATIONS AS SWEPT
BROWN INTO HIS BOUT OF PUSH AGAINST ANOTHER
SKIN ANONYMOUSLY OUTSIDE

Brown, invited to a party, went. He got in through the gate but
was accused of being a crasher. (The accusing one wasn't the
host who had invited him.) "Get out, you don't belong here,"
Brown found himself being commanded. "But White invited
me. Where is he, he'll tell you. *He* lives here, not you," said
Brown with logical stubbornness, holding his ground, refusing
to be pushed out. More guests arrived, the party was getting
very crowded. The crush pressed everyone against the walls
or against each other. No one was distinguishable from anyone else, as the massive human density became one congested
block conforming to the architectural contours of the apartment. Brown was mixed in with everyone else, and in the general scramble his identity became equally lost. He was immobile and pushed, unable to make his own path. He was packed
in with all the rest, and couldn't even maneuver his way to the
counter with the bottles on top and the glasses to be filled. He
was unpleasantly sober not yet having taken his first sip of party

beverage, and being sober was to be open to crowded unpleas-
antness that closed in around him from surroundings that inspired disgust for fellow men. "Whether I crashed or was invited, the party has only hemmed me in without release, I'm
stuck to this one room and there are other rooms equally tortured with population, a party is wrong to include so many
guests confined and gasping for their lost freedom. White has
been overpopulous a host and as a result he's generous to none.
It's hell to be in here but I can't get out. But my luck has turned,
for the mob has pressed me flat against this unflat girl I'm lean-
ing against as though tight in a dance with her locked in an intimate embrace. I find my head turned, she's so diverting. Our
eyes are close together, we're kissing our smiles. Everybody is
talking at once, the din is in such an uproar that *local* conversation is impossible for me to make myself heard above the general noise that makes one depraved ear of all this party. Now I'm
squeezed in with this girl, the contact is eloquent at our pure
body level on familiar terms so snug and economical in a compact harmony that speech between us couldn't append things,
any further than how far close we already are. Literally, we've
been thrown together in a sensuous collision and have become
stuck, and there's no hurry to unstick this accident with its nice
mating of parts. I feel like a whole man, being half of some little
something of which the other half is *her* as I appreciate it. She's
in no position to give me the brushoff, so I'm pressing home my
advantage and putting my most inflamed front forward, a pressure she can't retreat from or force back, indeed she meets me
halfway and urges me on with suggestive little pushes that purr
out her protruding encouragement that I persist now that her
resistance is being so obviously withheld. I make a pass at her
which she doesn't repulse nor consider forward nor presump-
tuous, such a pass we've come to at this stage of the game involuntarily arrived at. We lean toward maintaining this mutual in-

clination and keep on keeping it up now that our opposite paths have indeed converged in a clinch of total agreement that betokens such concord on behalf of having a common point of interest that touches on all else beside. Emphatically, there's hardly a need to put more stress to bear or rub it in any further. Front to front we face inward and keep pushing."

The party got out of hand. Everybody was stuck together, locked in like a frozen cubicle of jigsaws. No one could wedge an inch in or out. Brown and his new-met girl were by now plenty bored with each other. What each craved was privacy and solitude. Clearly, both goals presently stood impossible of achievement. What a huddled mass of people these were! Brown felt group-stripped of his individuality. He still was so sober! No relief from such intrusive surroundings.

The stuck-together blocks of ice began to crack, and cracking eased into melting, so soon the swarms scattered. People belatedly and angrily went home, though a few bored guests went tardily to the drinking tables to fill some merciful blessings to grace over the ordeal they had just gone through. White, the host, went around apologizing, from dispersing group to dispersing group. But he never reached Brown. Brown, dislodged from his inadvertent girl partner, tugged loose from her at last, had now lost sight of her and was rushing around to search her out and make an appointment for future contacts, for he felt suddenly nostalgic for her, being in the toils of her grip had contained some invaluable pockets of sensation and he wanted to assure the provision of their repetition with the same girl sometime soon for it would be a good habit to get into on a more voluntary basis than the first involuntary success. But he couldn't locate her in any of White's rooms. She'd gone home, and he'd not even found out her name? He'd give a description of her to White and White could supply him with her corresponding name and telephone number without which communication would be at a dead loss in the name of so far as her contact was concerned in Brown's plans to keep in regular touch with her to repeat the opportune stolen delights of this night's tightly-packed party. There, he discovered White, who greeted him.

Now to describe the girl and get her identification, for it was the host's duty to know the least of his guests even in so bulging a party given that some guests could have sneaked in without invitation or might have arrived having heard of it or shown up being told of it or went along in the company of those originally invited by hanging on or by being escorted and who all somehow got in to spread the walls out from inside and stretch the rooms bigger than before to accommodate hordes of that coinciding size. The world and a half appeared on that particular night to cram in at White's place. White felt responsible and must atone. Brown would put him through his paces concerning that intimate girl with the anonymous face. She should be singled out in particular by the description given, then be generally rounded up and singled out to be found, before Brown could engage her on their fine shoving match again.

"Of *course* she was pretty, Brown. *All* the girls I invite are bound to be pretty, girls like that give a party class, otherwise I'm amiss in my hostly duties. In particular, *how* was she pretty?"

But Brown had forgotten what the girl looked like. What a practical horror of omission this was, fatal for chances to find her. All he remembered was being pressed in *touch* with her, contact against her, but nothing visual had been retained. White shrugged, and couldn't help him, on such skimpy information, based on incomplete recollection. How unobservant Brown had been, with his body blindly feeling her and nothing but that to be recorded against the experience. Why should he deserve to meet her again, with such flimsy attention, and scant respect for her individual features? She was swallowed up in the merger of all girls in general that had the properties of bodies. So much for Brown's abortive romance, it's all over in that case, for it wasn't one case, it was all cases, that was his trouble, she'd been nothing special to him at all except as the waywardness of opportunity had set her to chance before his path in the surging impasse of the mob. Thus ended another chapter, a romantic escapade by mischance, in Brown's remorseless love life, ill-begotten by the gods of perchance and masked over in the vaguest of promiscuities without reference to the finer details that may have offered themselves in vain to Brown's insensitive skin that bruises but doesn't retain. His nameless girl friend was vanished, the one-shot proposition had now died to a faceless performance in memory's lustful ingratitude to a girl of uncertain identity. The Unknown Soldier has a grave; the unknown love lives on, having gravely faded from its time of origin as an unspecified commodity with its drift to the shoreless miscellany. So ends the story of what didn't matter to Brown. The value was never counted up, and the record is a scratch. He'd crash by invitation White's party again, when this same lifetime chances to circumstance its combinations to duplicate what exactly happened, people pressed together, an intimate encounter between strangers with rubbed-away evidence for the time thus closely spent in a consenting contact, a clash and a sundering, the flash that rubbed off and left no trace for the annals of sentiment. The skin takes on a mental friction, but with whom?

Title will follow *conclusion of this fiction.*

I

When I met Louise (and if I hadn't, where would this story be?), I thought discreetly inward, "So she's about to get divorced! And at such a young age! I wouldn't mind stepping right into her husband's place. Her figure makes me think of sex. If that's *her* figure, why not *with* her? It figures. But more than that, our minds meet. In some subtle way. Earlier at this gathering; when we were introduced by our mutual hostess among the early arrivals, we got to talking on a couch and the subjects flew by, one word led to the next, we ignored the other guests that kept coming in, and even our hostess herself, the rooms started to crowd up, guests standing in front of our couch pressed against our legs, a whole wall of shifting drinkers blocked our frontward view, but so immersed were we in each other it was as if we were on a desert isle with only coconuts and wild life other than the human oneness we were making. Barriers of re-serve were knocked down instantly, and we never had to resort to social etiquette that lay in wait if spontaneity failed. Formal manners and codes of decorum were like the Dead Sea Scrolls or Babylonian tablets, for all that they ever came in handy, for we had blended intimacies together and were lifelong friends an hour after meeting. Unknown to us, our hearts had traded places, like in an ideal movie romance, or so it seemed to me. Now I must ask her for *her* version, soon as she comes back from the washroom. This is the first time in my life I've ever been left alone by her. I hope it doesn't happen too often. She's already gotten to be a habit."

I loved Louise, right then. I needed her a bride, right away. I was in a marrying mood in a hurry. I had had enough of affairs that were always breaking up. I needed settling down. I wanted sex with Louise soon as possible, The gathering had swollen into a party. The place was mobbed. A lot of heavy drinking was going on. My own glass needed refilling. But I was glued to the spot on the couch where I had consolidated my lifelong relationship with Louise, who had suddenly happened to me. Her vacated place on the couch when she momentarily went off to the washroom was now pre-empted by someone nondescript in whom I hadn't the slightest interest, not even bothering to spend a side glance to ascertain what gender it belonged to. Louise had happened to me, and suddenly, in one great ripping motion, all the odd parts of my life, so incompatible before, had clicked into place, merging into an entire harmony. Life, in one swoop, had become complete. Its key was Louise. This event was the peak to my known existence. The chore of my remaining years would be to sustain a comparable level to the standard of what had befallen me now. Equipped with Louise as my constant woman by my side, I'd be equal to the current pinnacle enveloping me. I'd live up to it, by living it up with Louise, on whom I had committed a passionate dependency, by the involuntary circuit of surprise. I had come to this party intending to find a girl, but worldly cynical experience had held me back from hoping for the romantic impossibility of the miraculous forever. Bounded in by horizons, before of moderate prospects constantly qualified by reality, I was now spinning off into transparent and infinite openings, flying by opaque limits, expanding into the everywhere that was Louise. By the way, where was she? Twenty minutes ago she had gone off to the washroom and had yet to return. This is the longest I had ever gone without her, by fully twenty minutes: What a way to start off our life together!

As a man of action, I'd have to look for her. Seeing may be believing, but first comes looking. I stood up, and the vacated spot on the couch was instantly replaced by a now seated figure who started to paw with overtures the person who had taken the adjacent place (now a shrine, consecrated forever) occupied by Louise, who had vanished bafflingly and would have to be located. I checked the washroom and she wasn't its occupant. I'd scour the whole apartment, room by room. But all these dense people in the way! The clink of unending glasses! The glitter, the clatter. I would go off somewhere with Louise, somewhere remote, like a South Sea island (which my poverty couldn't even begin to afford), or more likely, to my bedroom however humble, or to hers better yet, since she said her husband had moved out and divorce proceedings were already in two law offices. Maybe her alimony would help to support us? I had no solid occupation, earning my living by the odd chance here and there, scrounging my rent-money through the haphazards of spasmodic employment, having no college degree or professional skill behind me. To justify this want of material ambition, I let it be proclaimed that my true field is philosophy, into which I delve whenever my idleness can afford the vacant moment. I'm writing an original philosophical book, that will tear the world apart. I've invented some brilliant but borrowed ideas for the occasion, and garbed them in my own literary style. Spinoza who polished lenses in Holland is dead, so I can easily take his place. But I hope *my* place isn't taken, in Louise's presumably unfickle heart? That idea worries me. I'll have to check and see. First to fortify myself, by filling anew my whisky glass at the improvised bottle bar, with an ice cube to convey solidity. I'd have to be at my best, in love's pursuit. Historically, it would be my second meeting with Louise. The first has gone into history, though yet unrecorded by bard or scribe, but registered in my bosom's thump of anxiety. Love notoriously has never had an easy time. I was to prove no exception. My goal was to make Louise mine. Her consent was vital, in this. I'd have to sound her out on her view. Were it to coincide with mine, then bliss. Were it no, then woe. Now, to the chase. Put off delay! Just go!

II

There I was, and the party was going full blast. I was already mildly intoxicated by force of whisky: but drunk totally on Louise. The role of the lover was mine to play, for its full blast was felt underneath the theatrical costume, deep within, mute, too realized as natural for performance to convey. Traditionally, I would die for her. But I could think of better delights. One was that she requited my love, and would make me her second husband at her girlhood years of twenty-two. I was more than ten years her senior. But no matter, for I made up for it, and then some, with an emotional immaturity that made me emotionally her junior, thus appealing to her youthful maternal instincts, which in purity were kept uncontaminated for me by her never having been a mother. She could start now, feeding me at her breast.

The goal, the goal, not to be lost sight of. Which is to gain the sight of my loved one. For that, to find her site.

My mission was clear. But what towered in the way? A forest of thick people-trees, swaying, interchanging, through which I could not see. Somewhere in their midst, or through their foremost ranks, was my hunt's prey. Must I roughly shoulder my way?

I looked here, I looked there. On route, I shouldered people, elbowed them, was jostled by them, collided with them, along a multi-mazed detour. The object was Louise. The chase was worth it. I mean her worth was worth staking pains over. I pondered on her. What little did I know of her? That she made me hot in the flesh was only too characteristic of her general gender, to whose faceless charms I was known to be prone. What distinguished Louise in *particular* from the rest? That she'd be youthfully divorced was scarcely unique for our shoddy times. I didn't know her wealth status, or lack of it. Her job, if any. Even where she lived. Or what her husband had done. Or what drove them to separate. Or even her last name: No, I was no Louise expert. But at *loving* her, I was adept.

Love's duty starts out with tracking down where she is. Will-o-the-wisp for my wild-goose-chasing? No, she was tangible. Let love seek out the way. This party was so jammed! People are stuck together, to arbitrary partners, not to chosen mates. I must have free access. The right of way is not easily granted, for the mob is obtuse, and wouldn't notice the frantic glaze in my eye, whose stars wouldn't rest till Louise was become beheld. Beheld, then held. Eyes have bodies behind them.

III

The search was fruitless. Like a demon possessed, tossing aside any offered cordiality, glad-handing, introduction, wave, or gesture by this assemblage of strangers and acquaintances, I had plowed my way circuitously with obsessive mania through this cluttered bewilderness of the infini-hydra-headed multi-complexitude of a party's disorganic motley whose dissonant pulse sprayed the anarchy at large which simply took place on scattered offshoots of no plan. The order to be made had to be my own, impressed by relentless will on this chaotic void of form. I looked for Louise eternally for two hours. Her invisible image glared at me ahead, while I plunged, lunged, and bumped. Angry objects in my way called me clumsy and worse. Every person turned into an obstacle, which I treated with impersonal impatience, while molesting their right not to have their surface jarred. I plowed into them. My ideal was hidden; the real was hideous. I hit out. I lashed forth. I became a blind momentum, a madness propelled in churning frenzy, oblivious to sensitive entities my hurtling would encounter. Rage gained me purple fury. I grew wilder than my wilderness in my way. I was a spectacle; and a livid hostess took hold of me and told me to get out. I had disturbed her peace and quiet, by disrupting the party's wildness with my own. It was *her* party, she was giving it, she must defend it, I must go. I was ejected, firmly. She helped me find my coat among an enormous pile that sagged the bed down. A couple were kissing under some of the garments, the lights were low in that bedroom. There was a rampage of high-blooded drinking. Violence was the cohesive force, but underplayed. Subdued murder scented the air. Was this a ritual Saturday outlet for tamely civilized souls? The big city was bulging with population. Its overflow had been invited here, while others just crashed it. The Sabbath hour had struck, but midnight formed no dividing line to temper the mood and moderate high spirits. The city in its decadence was here. The revolting illness of an age had come crawling in. Some guests had passed out; not me, I was thrown out. The hostess had her arm in mine, propelling me to the door. My madness had been for an object. The madness had undone me, with its object unachieved. "Wait!" I said, facing the hostess outside her threshold, her door half closed against my re-entry. "Where's Louise?"

"Who?" Her temper reflected the party's ugly mood. A dissolute riot was brewing. Snarling bodies, in the prevailing atmosphere, bred quick-snapping minds and branded venomous belligerence. My hostess seemed about not to cooperate. If anything, she would *wish* me thwarted. I had to combat this. I had to appeal to her humanity, The circumstances were adverse. My own urgency had to conquer them.

My hostage; middle-aged, stout, unmarried, was the occasional mistress of a married man, but had another boy friend on the side. She was an office manager in a fund-raising outfit that was suspected of shady dealings behind its facade as a charity set-up. I wouldn't trust her an inch. I must wheedle from her the vital information leading to Louise's whereabouts, or the love that was born tonight to change my life will have died on the same evening. Now survival rose to my cunning. I shook myself sober, and held on to my hostess by the fat of her upper arm under a ruffled blouse. I held on, to inquire.

"Get out, what do you want? I have to go back to see how my party is doing. Take your foot out of the door I want to slam. There's the hall and the elevator for you, use it. Who is this 'Louise' you want?"

"She's the one who . . ."

"Don't keep me standing here. The draft is entering with the door ajar. You're an intruder unwanted I want on out. You were rowdy in there, You were uncivil, now the party is out of hand. I blame you for the shambles of this party. I must assemble it somehow, I'm needed in there. Who were you looking for?"

"When I came early, you introduced me to Louise. Then she disappeared after a while. She had . . ." And I described Louise as best as my memory could, what she had on, her hair-coloring, her size, and other such inessentials. It was her soul I was in love with, not the outside. Frustration had spiritualized my love, on the sublimation principle. My dream was now an ideal's icon. Could my coarse hostess realize this? I insisted on remaining there, in the doorway, till the necessary disclosures were made. Courtesy was swiped away, where this imperative was involved. I would sacrifice pride too, and reasonableness, and gratitude. I'd undergo a whole overhauling, just to win back one more opportunity to woo tonight's met stranger, by the name of Louise. The hostess was shocked by this ardency that had swept me out of control. I touched a sympathetic nerve, among all that inhumane tissue. She'd get rid of me, but would have to satisfy me first. She braced herself, and delivered:

"Louise? You wouldn't want her. I advise you to change your goal, Her profession seems to be to make men into miserable swine. I've known her for years, my favorite niece was her best friend and constant school companion. Louise grew up into an ogre, that cut out men's hearts. I watched the development, she'd eat you out of your skin, two men were near to suicide because of her, some men broke down for grief, and all she is is twenty-two, and her past history has already piled up the corpses of formerly proud men, reduced to breathing shells with their cores mounted on Louise's trophy wall. I had an innocent lapse of mind in my unintended malice of introducing you to her; but resist the fatal pull, don't be drawn in like the rest of them, you've had a narrow scrape, desist from folly, I've given you the benefit of the wisest warning, be prudent to heed it, I'm not responsible for consequences otherwise. I should have kept her out of my party, for she strews trouble wherever she goes. But she got wind of it, since I'm not unknown, word got around, I couldn't avoid her coming. It could have been lethal for you. Vomit out your swallowed poison, and be luckily quits of her, unless you combine love with masochism, in which case it's hopeless, and you're undone, My biggest charity to you is to withhold her last name and all other details like her residence and so forth, especially her phone number that could tempt you. You almost contracted your bane of a disease that's destroyed better men then you, who went for her siren charms and had unhappy falls from their innocuous fortunes of before, enticed past curing. Don't go after your own plague and contrive a misfortune to join your woe to the victims she's collected. You feel hopelessly drawn, don't you? She's a horrid incubus to suck your vitals out, I mean a succubus, for it's men only she harms, you're naive if her reputation hasn't reached you, now go, leave my party, be grateful that she left long ago instead of claiming you as her next captive, but she threw you back into the sea, you were small fish for her, that's why she left early and didn't stick around. You don't know how kind I've just been to you. I showed you mercy to keep Louise's hooks off you; my depriving you is my saving you, if you knew what it is you seek. Now, haven't I been gentle? You're in my debt. I've known you only just enough to invite you as my guest. You were so close to catastrophe! Go home safe. Tuck your love for Louise away, and never let it be your folly to put it to serious action again. It's been the lesson of your life. Now kindly move your foot from the door. I have to rescue my party that's gotten out of hand. Let me return my attentions to it. Good night, and invent a prayer of gratitude, to me or God, that your love for Louise has led you only so far and then some merciful providence spared your disaster from finding Louise again. She left you unclaimed. Go out, while you're ahead."

The door closed, I was alone in the hall. Not to press my luck too far—that message stuck to me. But how far could the hostess be believed? As I said before, she was untrustworthy, She was known to practice deceit. She didn't often do good for people. Why would *I* just now be the exception? Should I believe her, or no? I'd have to investigate from a safe distance, for more findings. But it might get me wrapped up in the Louise hunt like a male fly in a female spider's web. That's the sort of danger to take care against. To get raveled up in that mess would be a complication it's well to guard against. I had been so desperate to marry Louise, so it would seem I had nothing to lose. In truth, I have much to live for. There's the book of philosophy I'm writing. If I play my cards right, it could lead to fame. Famous philosophers are very few in a century. The market is small. But I just might make it: Being spared from Louise, wasn't that a divine visitation to caution me prudence for my work ahead, without a ruthless interference? The female species of the race is known to be toxic. Louise, from my hostess's evidence if her testimony is to be given due credit, seems an extraordinary specimen of an already virulent species, and my valor would be to keep away, not draw near, for health and wholeness. Yet the magnet is tugging in me, to risk it. I'd rather die and be here, than live away. She's too intriguing; and safety is so pale and bland. Why live in a tepid, colorless vacuum, when I could seek out the spectacular morbidity, the violent, sinister, perverse, decadent romanticism of falling under her spell, and have the blessèd curse of her evil work to doom me low, and extract her diabolic sting for my own very skin! Mystery is life's finest gamble, though the odds go against. My downfall would have some drama behind it. I will have lived. Let Louise be *life's* source, however the penalty. It would be a *vital* death for me, on a poignant stage of agony; it would give some definition to my blank, some highlight and relief to this blob of my amorphous life if unleashed to lurch by the violent tide of a Louiseful of drowning. Let me go under. Such fatal attractions are divine. Doom is sanctified. It's a sort of glory I can't get otherwise. It's my only outlet from pallor, from the mediocrity of deluding myself that I'm an original philosopher—there would be no consolation if I fail. Why play it safe and dull? Louise is exciting. Love is beckoning. It's exerting its pull on me. I have something to die for. Better a posthumous life, than none at all. My own destiny has sounded. It's like the call to war, Why resist what tests nature to its noble challenge? I'll go. Louise is my destiny. I'll greet my scourge. Her *willing* victim, I'll be. I've *chosen* it: Free will. I'm not a clod. I have drive and vigor. I'll donate it all to Louise. She preys on it. I'll go under. Love is a heady cause. It perks up things brisker, the air flows swift, it ejects my stale torpor. I'm *me*, this way! I have a being to become. I'll go off to joust in the tournament. Glory will befall me. What a fall to be worthy of! To achieve my undoing by Louise, is playing life at its high stake, and to take Tragedy by anticipating it, since it arrives anyhow, only I precipitate it; why should it delay? I'll take the day by storm. And undergo an early night.

IV

I would let my enchantress tempt me; Let her do her worst! It would be converted to my best, under a boisterous sky of heroism.

The hero's role I've never played. To do it fully, it must be tragic, Louise is compliant on that. She visits tragedy upon men. That's her native talent. But am I blowing this up? I've taken the hostess's word, coupled to my passionate only interview with Louise herself. The hostess may have distorted things, to mislead me. Love is enough for misleading, without a lying tongue beside. But what motive would the hostess have, in telling me what she did? I still don't trust her. It's a thick mystery I'm in, by grace of love, which put me in the way of caring. Were love not there, what would be the fuss about? It moves me. Was Louise a mirage? I had sat on the couch with her. It was *seeming* hallucination, but it really happened.

I'm still hanging around in this hall. I'm ignoring the elevator. Guests keep leaving the party and go down the elevator. Very *late* guests sometimes come up to enter. Or are they crashing it, having heard about it late? So people pass me by in the hall, ignoring me. I'm lurking here in the shadow, I ignore *them*. I want another attempt at Louise, to tempt danger at full strength. I have to think back. I have to reconstruct. Louise said she was going off to the washroom, then I never saw her again. Why hadn't she ever returned, when she knew I was waiting for her? It seemed to have been a sacred promise, she certainly seemed to care, our hearts had taken a vow of twin destiny, I'm sober now so I can remember, this is no drunken rant. It happened, what happened is history. I have to go by it, history must be obeyed, it leads us. But what I want to know is where did

Louise go off to, if it were with a man she picked up or who encountered her as the party filled up. Was she abducted, perhaps? Kidnapped, and waiting for me to rescue her? Is her love for me deep, as mine is for her? I'm haunted thinking thus. I've got to act.

I kept loitering at the end of the hall. More and more guests were leaving. No one was straying in now; in denser groups, they were all going. In packs, they descended the elevator. I malingered, wondering. I'd have to question everyone I knew on Louise. Some leaving guests recognized me, they knew me. One was a very close friend of the hostess, and he was very social, so much so that his range of acquaintances penetrated every circle in this concentrically sociable city. His knowledge would expand as far as Louise, I knew that. So I buttonholed him, I streaked out of the shadow where I was suspiciously "hiding", to greet this vital source or information. He had a girl friend with him, but that wouldn't stop me. I pumped him, going down the elevator with him. It yielded good results. He knew *of* Louise all right, but didn't know her. He'd help me with as much information as he could give me, to the end that I would be able to locate Louise. He guaranteed that tomorrow— or later today, dawn now approaching on its wintry schedule— he'd put me in possession, through his extensive string of connections, of Louise's whereabouts, her phone number, her husband's name, her situation, her history, anything I wanted to know within knowing. He's good at that sort of thing. His occupation, in fact, is that of journalist. He's used to snooping and sleuthing, to dig things up. He used to be a court reporter covering criminal cases. He knew every detective's method. He'd be of grand use to me, feeling generously inclined, and sympathetic to my being love-smitten. "Someone in love should always be helped out: he's in a precarious, vulnerable state, and mustn't be left to suffer," said my benefactor. As for the hostess, my benefactor confirmed my suspicion against trusting her. She was generous in giving parties, but deceitful as a person, with a decided edge in malice. My benefactor would set me straight. I'd go by what *he* finds, not by what my hostess suggests. "But not now," said my benefactor. He wanted to be alone with his girl friend. They were both tired from a long night of drinking. (I was walking with them on the street to the subway stop.) My benefactor and his girl friend wanted to go to sleep now. They'd warm themselves in each other's arms before drowsing off. It was the age where marriage wasn't necessary to end a night this way. So he'd help me no longer now, except in promising me that were I to call on him later that (Sunday) night, he'd be fresh and able to help me. A time was set, and I scribbled down his address. I'd have to wait till then, for satisfaction. Meanwhile, I should go home and sleep. I had only recently, in the night that just was (the sun was rising), fallen in love. With whom? I'd know later that night. He ducked into the subway, taxis being scarce at that hour, with his girl friend falling asleep on his shoulder. I was within walking distance of my own poor apartment, in the outskirts of my own slum. I grunted good-night, and walked home. I felt hope. I rose to heroism. Louise would be tracked, and found. Whatever she'd turn out to be, even if the hostess had been right about her, I'd marry her, even to my ruin. It was *my* life: Doomed to be destroyed. Why not by me?

I'd be killed by Louise. Is there a more privileged way to die? Love is a heightened value of the loved one. The value I put on Louise is very high. How deep is love? Its greatest extent is to die for it. Then I'm game. I'll give myself in. I have high taste. *Any*one can die. But to join *Louise's* elite? That's a club, though, that's growing less exclusive all the time, if the hostess said right. I'd be only *one* member of many? Then as *I* die, I'd become the last, by carrying my killer down to keep my company in the hell of our design. That's *rich* choice! That's for keeps!

V

In her choice company, so select. *With* her. Not without. With. To be with her. Love wants to be with. With the one loved. That's to balance desire with goodness. It's good to be with the one loved. Alone apart is bad. I've got to close the gap.

Who knows what Louise is? Love knows only itself. Love is lonely, without the one loved. Louise was created by me, when I found her. Love drew her lineaments. Love can't do without her. Will the real Louise please step forward? You're needed. I must control it so that you're mine. Otherwise, the pain in the void.

I wait. I wait long. Her arrival in my life is by my arrival in hers. I've got to go get her. She's *there*, somewhere. I must be there, too, when she is. That's to put up a good opportunity. Then, the thing in my mind that is *her* can go up against the thing in *real life* which is her. To pit truth against truth. Two truths: inside and outside. Both of them are Louise. The Louise in my head lives for *me*, The one in real life—couldn't she *also* live for me? That's to make it a *real* ideal. Does life contain it? Can this miracle be spread out to outstretched length and still not burden impossibility to reply "Outlandish!"? Miracles are quiet, they take place. Let *mine* so be. The Louise as she is, and the one I'm thinking of—let their powers converge, and they both become one! With me in the middle! I'm there!

VI

I'm David, as a name. The "benefactor" I'm on my way to consult for information as to the whereabouts of a person of interest to me, Louise, is Stephen. He's known to be a close friend of last night's party hostess, Jane, But why is Stephen, the journalist, Jane's close friend, if he warned me against trusting her, terming her deceitful, malicious, downright destructive? Why would he remain her friend, in that case? I hardly knew Jane myself, though enough to be invited to that rather fateful party. Stephen doesn't know Louise, but knows *of* her, and knows how to find out more. For me, the primary priority in all this mustn't be lost sight of. My love for Louise, whom I only met last night, must be advanced to the point where I'm *with* her again. I've had too much of *mulling* over her, in endless hopes and theories, in dreary rounds of endless doubts, the treadmill of love running in hope's gamut. She hasn't been out of my mind. I've still hardly slept yet. I've got to objectify this inwardness; to locate, court, woo and win the corresponding Louise of my dreams. Taking action is the step. So I'm on the subway to visit Stephen, who'll open gates for me. How many gates need opening, for one Louise to enter my arms? I'm on my way into the world. That's where the real Louise is. My love will be objective and real, turned outward into contact with her on an actual talking level, holding her hand—but again, it's my imagination talking. Can't I shut it up? It hasn't ceased since the meeting with Louise. Outside reality has to balance it out, to prevent imagination from becoming a swollen tyrant. All I want is to get Louise. And imagination isn't enough.

Stephen is associated with *reality*. He's a journalist, he digs up facts. I'm relying on him. Not on Jane, the lying hostess who warned me off Louise for my own good. But if she did lie, why *that* lie? How would it serve her? She said Louise destroys men who by falling for her come into her power. Stephen has got to straighten this out. He's my fact-finding commission. Knowledge is wisdom. That would make love effective, give it power to act well on its behalf. The attainment of Louise is the goal. In my mind today I was ready to die for her. I'm in her spell. Now,

I'm ready for *her* to be in *my* spell. That would be love *lording* it, proud and arrogant. Not love submissive, abject, rendering itself powerless by turning itself, and all its would-be power, into the hands of the loved one, whose arms are thereby increased, with total mastery over the loving one: and the loving one would then willingly die. No, that's no manhood for me! Where's my human dignity? I'll gain Louise's respect. The solution is for her and me to love each other equally. But here I am, dreaming again, scheming a practical ideal. Given half a chance, my mind runs off that way. Love had rendered it giddy. In this frame, I can't trust my mind. So I'll borrow *Stephen's* level head, who'll do my forceful thinking for me on *reason's* stable ground. That way sooner reaches Louise. Who I *won't* die for, nor will she for me. Love will be our golden mean, in equality.

Love is thought of as domination, or being dominated. Love is willing to abase itself, or to gain the masterful ascent. Why one or the other, ruling or being ruled? That's emotion running to extreme. Reason pleads love's equality. So let it be. I'll grant Louise hers; and she mine.

I'm being fair. I'm more of mind, less of heart, Here's where I get off, Stephen's subway stop. I exit the opening doors, up the steps, out to the street. I've memorized the address. I walk a few blocks. Here's the apartment building. I ring the outside bell, and an electronic signal from Stephen's apartment makes the building door receptive to my opening it. I've passed my first hurdle like a true citizen of the city, and now the elevator opens for me, and up I'm going, to alight on Stephen's floor. I knock on his door, also ring his bell, for I'm simply eager. The door is opened by Stephen. In the room is his girl friend who left the party with him. One other person, other than her and Stephen, is there. I'm noticing who. I see her, I look. She's wearing a new dress. But it's the person I want. Her name is Louise. I had fallen in love with her the night before. Now I see her. Reality is strong, in this light. It rubs out my love. My dream has faded. The *real* Louise is there. A sun puts out the candle.

Louise is more staggering than her image; Stephen bids me sit down, I'm tottering. His girl friend goes into the kitchen to make coffee. We all drank too much the night before to drink now. We're all sober. I'm *too* sober. Louise is blinding. She's sitting on that chair. I'm on this one. Stephen is on the couch. I'm losing control. The dreams had protected me. I'm going under now, for the dreams have burst. The presence of Louise has too much might and force. I can't digest it in one sitting. I'm now in a *real* trance, out of my isolation. Louise is happening to me in the flesh. Why is she here? Stephen had invited her? But he hadn't known her. He found out how to contact her, and did. He did this for me. But I can't handle it. I'm not equal to it. I'm sinking. Love is not for this world. Love is in me, so neither am *I* for this world. This world that contains Louise. This Louise-containing world. I blank out. Stephen must have carried me to the couch. He's attending on me, his girl friend is pressing a damp sponge on my forehead. I'm revived enough to see that Louise is still on her chair, which is now turned in my direction on this couch. She's observing me. Is there compassion?, or what?, on her face. I can't see that face. It's too bright. I turn away. I feel inadequate. Love makes people weak. I'm being seen in my weakness. Will she scorn me?

I'm not being seen to advantage. I'm putting up a contemptible appearance. But maybe Louise *thrives* on giving out sympathy to a deserving victim. But what makes me deserving? Is my love for her a *virtue* in her eyes? If it is, I'm in luck. If not, then perversity dogs me, and ill fortune will happen to all my emotions. I try so hard. I'm too helpless to try.

VII

I hadn't slept after going home from the party this morning, Sunday. Now it's Sunday night, I'm on the couch in someone named Stephen's apartment. When had I last slept? (I'm sleeping now, I think.) The party was Saturday night, and I woke up early on Saturday morning. During the day I did some philosophy research for this project or exposition or thesis or treatise or major work I'm in the process of. It has to do with the realm of the mind. But the subject is too obscure to define. It's bogging me down. I don't know where I'm going. That's what's so hopeful. You see, if I *did* know where I'm going, it would be only a mediocre product of the conscious mind, with a known, foreseeable conclusion—not a great solution from deeply probing at the unknown. I'm in the dark, so there's hope, and I'm looking for the light. This is what I'm engaged at, in my philosophical inquiry.

I'm not in love with Louise now. I once was, not long ago—a few minutes ago I saw her in person, in this room. Now I'm out on the couch. Stephen and his girl friend are poring over me, solicitously. The chair Louise was on before is empty now. Where has she gone *this* time? It puts me back in mind to the party. The couch was empty where she had sat and we had, I thought, traded hearts. Then her absence grew longer, and I did my stubbornest to resist—I mean oppose—that increasingly terrible absence. But I couldn't undo it, the absence. Then I enlisted Stephen's help, that's why I'm here tonight. Yet where am I? I feel like I was *always* here, that Louise had *always* just became absent. That's a sort of trauma, trapped in time. A habit of the trauma-trapped mind. Was its archetype a birth-fright? Anyway, I succumb. I'm nowhere: where I want to be. My mind is off. It's off me, I'm off it. It's a leave-taking, for a duration, between the mind and me, The *mind* was the one that dwelled on Louise: not me. I'm left, with the mind gone. Louise has left too.

Did she go out *with* my mind? She went *off* with my mind? Then should I be jealous of that mind, which has wound up with the desired Louise, while I lie here with neither? No, for the *mind* loved her, not I. So *I* can't be jealous, if *I* hadn't loved her. But is this mere hair-splitting? Maybe, but imperative. My life is on it, my split life. Have I gone out of my mind? Turned insane? Clinically speaking, schizophrenia technically? How can I tell, if I'm *undergoing* it? What is knowledge?

Back to my work-in-progress of philosophizing. I'm trying to discover the mind. Twenty-four hours ago, *love* occurred in my mind. Since then, I was like a man possessed, and now I'm a man drained, loose of the obsessed image. Why did it leave? Louise left, it left. The image and the object. I'm left. Where is the mind, where is me? Who is happening? I'm in Stephen's apartment. He and his girl friend have put blankets over me, pillow under me, and left me to retire on the couch all night. They're in their bedroom. Does she *live* with him? The morals are loose, since man was invented. That's why man had to invent marriage.

VIII

Outside it's winter. The howling window is black. My coat is hung up in the closet. I'm under the blankets on the couch. The lights are out. But the shades are only partly drawn; I can see a street glow diluted on the exposed window. It eerily penetrates "my" room.

Louise has vanished? I *did* see her. She was actually in this room, only this night. Now it's on the Monday morning-side of midnight.

I'm floating away, or on air. My mind is light. But I said before that my mind *left* me. So what is it doing *with* me? Then it never *did* leave. But did Louise?

The solution to my philosophy: The mind dwells inside, Louise outside. Louise is a free agent. She left a dent on the mind, which dictates it to *me*, in a relay that transforms it. So Louise has occurred to me third-hand, sort of. First-hand is the real Louise, as she is. Second-hand is the Louise received by my mind, and the mental repercussions during her prolonged absence. Third-hand is the passing on by the mind of its Louise-image to me. So Louise is mine, at a remove; or at twice removed. It would be practical of me to take pains to meet her again. But I feel so passive! I'm out on the couch, but still thinking. It avails me in circles, nowhere.

I'll sublimate this predicament into its proper place, a philosophical work. An irresolvable problem gets transformed, with corresponding compensation, into the work of a mind and words. I'll put it systematically, and it will be a break-through in original philosophy. I'll be a celebrity within restricted circles who have a head for those things. I'm game for it. Louise was my *material*. Love made her so. Then the hostess Jane's warning me on Louise's danger, and Stephen my journalist benefactor's optimistic skepticism over his friend Jane's veracity and his refuting the good faith in her motives. And me arriving here, with Louise here, it was unexpected, now she's gone. Life is so thought-provoking! Thought uses *people* to complicate itself. Of course, love motivated thought. Love moves the world. It's the incentive for the sun, and the other stars: they immediately go out, once there's doubt. Love remains, it lingers behind, joins with doubt, enters contemplation. Contemplation can be in a speculative, theoretical, halting cast. I falter, and turn firm again. Louise and philosophy are the same thing. I'm free, knowing that.

IX

It's morning, tra-la. The light in the room is from nature. Stephen and his girl friend have their coats on, they're about to leave to their respective places of work. Stephen says I should stay here, for I'm not well, I need to rest in a warm piece. The girl friend has a substantial breakfast kept hot in a metal container waiting for me in the kitchen. Stephen bids me take it easy. Why not? It's easy to do.

I'm comfortable, I rest. My host and girl friend have gone. Then I remember the word Louise. A proper noun, someone's name. It's the remnant of my love. I *really* need a rest. Love has worn me out. On such little nourishment: The imagination did the trick. It took up the slack of Louise's being gone so often.

Speaking of Louise, who is she? Who, as well, are Jane, and Stephen, and Stephen's girl friend? I'm David, and there's hope for me. For I've just thought of Louise in context with other people, in "the same breath" with them. That puts her, sort of, in her place; consigns her *to* a place. She was so *out* of place before. She had topped the world, and reduced its other inhabitants to relegated hiding places with inanimate things. She really took over, but brutally. Not so now. I'm recognizing what happened. I'm undergoing a perspective-restoring retrospect, which at last recognizes proportion. Louise had overwhelmed proportion, exploded it entirely. Now, she's a vehicle for promoting thought. I'm gaining headway.

But where?, anywhere? What am I led to? To oblivion? That means love's end. I'm cured.

But is being cured so good? What *is* good? *Breakfast* is good, so I go in the kitchen and eat it. Now more energy floods into my mind, and I'm well rested, too. Stout Jane, the party hostess, is now the subject of my dwelling. Why is she friends with Stephen, who lives here? Another tireless inner monologue occurs, based on these, moved around by love, with Louise dead.

I'm in a mental tedium. *Why* is Louise dead? Because I once *did* love her. Not now.

What *is* now, but this? But this, what is *this*? This is where I am? I go around, on the circular head. When my head falls off, I can examine its thoughts and see how they were dominated by love: so thoroughly. Was Louise a vehicle for love, by which love entered? And where has love gone? Will I see Louise again? *Is* there a future? What is future, what is time? What is contained in the head? Where is thought, and why does it change? What is love, what does it do to the mind? How is it based on a real person, to what extent? Thus I cogitate. I'm a *born* philosopher. I love wisdom, and life. Life and wisdom love back. They Louise me.

(Full title, now that story has ended:)

AN UNSOLVED LOVE STORY, WITH AN UNSATISFACTORY END, WHICH LEADS OUTSIDE FICTION AND POSES THE PROBLEM UNANSWERED ON LOUISE CENTRALLY, WITH SOME MINOR QUESTIONS TOO, AND IS IN THE FIRST PERSON. BUT, IS IT TRUE? WE'RE TOLD NOTHING: ACTION WAS OVERWHELMED BY THE THOUGHT IT LED TO, IN THIS HERO'S MIND. THAT'S WHERE LOUISE WAS, IN HIS MIND. OUTSIDE IT, SHE KEPT PERPETUALLY DISAPPEARING, SO THAT SHE LEFT THE STORY BEHIND, WHICH COULDN'T KEEP UP. THUS IT LIMPS, TEETERS ON UNCERTAINTY, AND BECOMES THE MENTAL SHOWCASE FOR A NARRATOR WE CAN'T CREDIT, OR IF WE DO, THEN IS LOUISE BELIEVABLE? SHE'S LOVED BY THE NARRATOR, HER IMAGE FADES, SHE DOES A DIVE-OUT, AND THOUGHT REMAINS. PHILOSOPHY IS LEFT HOLDING THE BAG. WHAT TO DO WITH IT? WHAT'S IN IT? *WHAT* BAG? LOUISE, AND STRAY CONTENTS, FALL OUT OF

THE BAG TURNED UPSIDE DOWN; ONCE THEY DO FALL, THE HERO-NARRATOR HAS NO MORE LIFE EXCEPT THE PAGE OF FICTION, WHICH AESTHETI- CALLY COULDN'T ROUND OUT WHAT IT ROLLED UP TO, AND THERE WE ARE, LEFT OUT. WE CAN'T FOL- LOW. IT'S OVER.

IN THE PAST I HAD A FUTURE WIFE. NOW, SHE'S MERELY A PAST GIRLFRIEND.

At a party you meet fabulous people—I mean fabulous. (At another party you don't so much. But why go into *that*, at this time? It spoils my whole point.)

For example, I met a girl who later became my own wife. Later still, she became my estranged wife. Finally, what she is now—my ex-wife,

But at the time, at the party, our entire future, together and apart, was unknown. We *met*—and went on from there.

If it hadn't been for the party. . .

If it hadn't been for her. . .

If it hadn't been for me. . .

If it hadn't been for nature. . .

However, what happened, happened. It's undeniable, but it did.

Yesterday, at a party, I met my new future wife. But does *she* know it? I must gradually bring her around to espousing my point of view, before she can espouse me.

But will she, in the even *further* future, become my *estranged* wife? And then, even further than that, my second ex-wife? I apprehend that she may follow the pattern of my *already*-ex-wife. But it won't be a *duplicate* process, I hope. How can it be? This new woman is different from my ex-wife, and I'm different from the ex-me-self. So what will be? Courtship, wooing, from me. Anticipated acceptance, from her. *Then* what? It's an unknown future—open, unfilled out. Time will, of course, tell.

Time *has* told. It's already, now, years later. That anticipated second wife turned out different than I had hoped for, to the point where not only did she reject me for her husband, but I

lost interest and didn't even propose. So we "broke up" after just a short romance, and permanently retired into separate separations. Just as well. I never *did* like her, anyway.

That last statement-sentence, that I never *did* like her, anyway, is said by me in retrospective interpretative review, long after the fact, and represents a distortion from the hindsight of Now. Of *course* I liked her—how, otherwise, could I have projected my plan for her to become my second wife? So, I'm playing loose with the past, in the narrow perspective of analysis. I'm in a new state, now. It determines the way that I look back. The past is merely my material, to justify present concerns, current indifferences, new aspects of outlook. The past is my plaything. It will conform, to my immediate goals of purpose, by supporting what I now want, and by playing silent and absent background in its points of irrelevance to that which is newly active in me. I, thus, fashion the meanings of the layers of my past, to molds of my improvised plans, the next waves in my future.

JUST IN PASSING

The street is where strangers pass each other and never meet. Sometimes they even look at each other—in passing—and one may wonder about the other one's life.

But then they pass out of each other's life. And out of each other's mind.

In parks, stations, buses, trains, thoroughfares, stores, all public places—in passing, they pass by. They're all on their way to meet people they're going to meet—deliberately planned, arranged meetings. But in passing, they pass by other people— some of whom they could have known, and loved. Who can tell?

But shyness, reserve, guardedness, not taking any chances, distrustfulness, suspicion, reticence, minding one's own business, keeping one's distance, not venturing to presume, going one's own way, behaving in an orderly public manner, civility, self-containment, unforwardness—we're trained not to disrupt or bother other people. Even the ones who, if we only knew them, would play significant roles in our lives. But we'll never know—or know *them*.

The meetings went unmade. They were the non-meetings. The meetings that never were. They just never took place.

But they *could* have been major events: some of them.

But they never hatched. They died, as mere embryonic possibilities. With further development fully stunted.

Passing by so many people. All those others' lives. Actual lives—unrealized by us.

Their lives are going passing by. Overlapping glimpses, just caught, in passing.

Well, we're stuck with the ones we *do* know. But we get unstuck, too, when we want to.

Other people, in our own lives. That's what *we* are, to *them*, *too*: *also* "other."

We're all each other's others. A whole community network, of others—in the flux of casual confusion, in the random of our going.

The people, passed by: Whom we pass by. The passed-by people. The never-agains.

All you strangers. I seem to know you. In *general*, only, by supposition. In particular, no. You're all my lost strangers. The unfound non-people of my life. I guess into you, by the ones I *do* know. That's not fair to you—to be hazarded a guess at, as to your beings, on the basis of people I know but whom you don't.

You're then my unknowns. You're always there—in your assorted changing shapes—but never clinched into knowing.

All the passing. The crossing of paths. The shifts, the displacements. All that irregularity. All those unfilled-in forms. Gone and replaced. The going is constant. An endless procession, of every which way. Sometimes, I stare: or catch you staring. Caught, in being interested. Browsing, window-shopping—just curious. The vague wonder. Who are *you*? And *you*? Your outside shapes pass. And I'm one to you—if you even look.

There are too many. We grant them all a wide berth. Too many, those publicly promiscuous samples, all going by.

Whom may you be? If I knew you, would I even care? If so, how much?

My multi-faced stranger. Floating, up there.

WHAT CAN BE MISSED BY WASTING A WEEKEND IN THE COUNTRY'S NATURAL BEAUTY WHILE MEANWHILE A SUDDEN PARTY HAS MUSHROOMED IN THE CITY, BEARING PERISHABLE BLOOMS IN THE ROMANTIC CULTIVATION OF ONE SATURDAY NIGHT

You missed all the excitement! There was a big party!

Oh! *(Disappointedly:)* I was away in the country! What happened? Were there girls available?

They were piled on top of each other, unescorted, without dates. Just *panting* for guys to stop the hole up their legs.

Sounds utopian.

The most accidental opportunity imaginable! Ideals of incredible purity. *My* cock alone accommodated three of them that night and the next. Now it's all sheathed in a numb bandage.

I envy you for what you had to do to achieve your convalescence. And *I* was admiring the green scenery in a dull country estate, during a weekend that erotically was an absolute nullity, with trees and birds hovering in a passive overhead. Oh summer void! Meanwhile, you were honorably acquiring the wounds of manhood, heroically braving those gallantly numerical odds with your defiant male solitude. I would love to have stuck my own bulge into your lucky pants, and plant my pole of defense. What age engendered their lovely beauty?

All in their twenties, from a variety of fetching looks, with dresses rising to the crunchy writhing, and long legs dangling their wide assets. I was inspired for life!

(Anguished:) Oh, could *I* only have been there!

You sure *should* have been, and others too! An *army* would have gone away happy! Every sofa boasted a posy of girls, armchairs thrilled to their thronged stuffings, settees lounged in fulfilled settings, divans delved divine to sprout a glorious harvest of bottoms, davenports sprung deep thighs in engaging foreshortenings, floor cushions teemed with critically raised knees, footrests rooted a nested bevy of soft mushroomings, couches wore a crossed array of anonymously stunning legs curled to the wildest curvature that the bones underneath would permit, and beds galore poignantly perfumed a pose of reclining hints. Oh queasy clutch of delirium, oh hallucination-veiled Real! They were so much *there*, that hunting would have rushed past and raised redundant waste. No haste, for those cosy offerings!

(Tortured:) And my idle chastity in the country!

The wrong place's poor timing by a lost fool! You missed the creamy helping of all parties! Girls beyond counting, the pay-off prey to all our prayers! The reaped amplitude of abundance, but with no devalued quality for all that superfluous quantity! Heaven casting its permissive fire on earth's mold of lust, for a few stray princes of privilege!

And not *me* there! Oh what a deathly absence!

You beggar in the kingdom of misfortune!

Oh let me grovellingly persuade you to divulge how it was.

Not a bad bit of plentiful worthwhile! No lack of a great lot of girls disproportionately amounting to an overwhelming total of the comparative people there. I knew what the score was, and I speculated my spectatorship for the stakes of participation. And was paid in the lascivious coin of gratification!

Oh muscular master ripe for action at the right spot in the full tides of chance showering the gods' favor: At the helm seize the multiple-y offered advantage at your male mercy of disposal!

And rarely just a few miscreants to share this bounty with, the gifts by goddesses of their own divine countenances to a spare crew of mortal self-helpers there, men normally of meager circumstance, now basked in blessings most promiscuous.

And I not included! Oh deep exclusion!

And vastly unbalanced the sides were, with girls expiring for their non-mates! A generous vacuum, where men should have been!

Oh so slaughtered as a retroactive absentee am I in remorse for having been away, as regret salvos forth a wailing tide of sobs for my backfired opportunity till now I was ignorant of! The haunting ghost of my non-appearance! Oh to recapture that coveted time, to clutch the *present* of that hour whose virginity re-opens for my welcomed grab and consumed ravishing, should *now* reprieve me from omission's tardy offense to deal me swift commission now and dispatch the mission home! The ignorant neglect of before, made good in savage recompense, now. And give time its just requital, paying interest in belated debt thereof.

A pity you weren't there; it would have been well worth your while.

Oh my wiles weren't foreseeing, enough; or prophecy would have turned calamity into paradise, by taking an early train home from the country instead of the fruitless loitering under the heavy age of boughs on trees surrendered to Saturday's troubled dusk brooding elsewhere the event to be at, for in the big city this fateful party took place.

I was there; were you?

No, I missed it.

And *what* you missed will rankle to infinite magnitudes, corrupting your conscience and destroying your tranquility, in your mangled war-torn thoughts projected on the disastrous screen of forever.

My misfortune is that I can't reclaim the chance again; the fortuitous coincidence of incidents brings about such a party just once; those who didn't attend may never ever attend, in all retrospective torturings.

The party is over. It so happens that you missed the boat.

Among the guests, the pretty girls monopolized?

As previously implied. Why there weren't as many *guys* there, to match 'em all up, though beyond my comprehension, was not beyond my opportunism. I could pickingly choose in a widely assorted selection. But I was too sought to be too seeking. *Occident*ally, I became *orient*ed to a harem by no means in*sultan* to the most fastidiously pampered of lechers!

I die post-mortemly at the party I never was at. My consciousness returns, to reconstruct an event whose occurrence was uncreated at the time it happened, it so happening that I was away at the time, uninvited, unnotified, unreminded, unheeding, unavailable. Green inactive vistas were my serene country musing. My manhood's prime was galloping away, while your beats of virility were busy pursuing the scent! While I was slumbering in natural surroundings of leafy hill, grassy dale, and meandering brook, overhung by pastoral cloud conducted to the purple sunset slaughter: your passion was being artificially stimulated in simulated conditions by a socially prepared party that provided a man-made setting for those encounters legitimized by the accepted convention of privately foregathered assemblage brought gregariously together by the host's momentarily spurred improvisation for a last-minute, open-housed invitation to those spontaneously and informally available of acceptance. The unplanned arrivals, with preponderously feminine predomination, began to pour in, skirts rustling deliciously and a helpful of lipstick pre-kissing each mouth. You among them like a lording lion, and I bound unsuspectingly to country innocence.

Surely your spirit must definitely have been there, in heart representing your oblivious proxy distantly delegated. However, to attain to full guest-privileges such as drinks and pre-sex romance, you had in body to be there by personal presentation; a mere mental premonition wouldn't do, however accurate its identification by a far mingling of harmonious essences hooked up in the sympathy of recognition by mystic strands of union in sensory subterraneousness on the electric circuits of the air. The fact is that you were absent.

Had I known!

Only, you didn't know, and you were actually deprived, because unapprized, of those prizes men thrill to be surprised by in tilting enterprise. Even as a spy, you put in no presence.

No, I didn't show up. I've got to admit it. What was I where, concurrently to that?

Your soul was contemplating a rustic heaven; but in the big town, the girls were for the having. Had you only made the scene!

Had I, I would have made it ob-scene.

You would had to have seen it, ob-servingly.

From you, I've *heard* it.

Absurd to have heard, when obscene to have seen. I'd say you missed out!

Looks like I did. Can I make it up?

It won't happen again. Too late.

Well, and the girls are fled. How many phone numbers did you capture?

More than I could use. Three I possessed so far, with dates lined up for advance months nocturnal appointments ahead. An endless stud to a fresh nightly partner infinitely renewed!

And the party was the source to your new-found wealth?

Yes, all owing to Saturday night's mimed pre-orgy.

Could I have a share? Can you donate your surplus to me?

That would cancel out your being absent, reprieve your sentence of punitive abstinence, and acquit you of your negligent crime altogether. To be rewarded, you had to *arrive*. Why should I tilt the scales of fortune, by arbitrarily intervening in your distressed deprivation and depriving you of the consequence of being unfortunately absent? I don't like to interfere with the way life's chance operates. To relieve your lonely gloom would be sentimentally to meddle in fate's harsh affairs. Life's rigor is tough; why should I disrespect this iron law by softly rushing to your aid? Luck was good to me mainly by contrast to yours. Any selfish priority exceeds friendship's mythical bonds of implied obligation. I risk the blatant hatred of your envy's enmity. I won't nullify reality's process, in your dismal case. I won't reverse the way things turned out. Your lesson must stick; and let misery be your lot, and mine be the splendor of many shared lusts spun in rotation upon the central sameness of my one rod as their common symmetrical axis, the revolving wheel's dominant male focus, the needle of steeled durability. Survival has chosen me, to thrive; you lost a party, and your life must be denied. A fair segregation between my elation and your stern, irrefutable negation. Your male factor is done; mine, newly won. Unequal rejoicing for me, exultant in triumph, as a cock's seed-sewn crow; and you, you're irony's sacrifice to the lack of justice anywhere. Earth's scheme has a plotless design, ruining or rewarding on the slightest turn. Do you expect another country-invitation?

If I get it, I won't accept.

But why not companion the natural glory there, the wholesome purity of the outdoors that consoles many a forlorn heart?

My *own* nature forbids it, a lesson I've instinctively learned in peril of acute pain upon the intolerable circumstance of my return to discover what beyond recall I missed. The country is celibacy's seat, and virtue's dubious setting of innocent solitude pendulant from green branches near a twittering birdcall. A dull boon at best, a dreary monk's-world. Society is the free sexual opportunity for all cultivated folk. A country weekend breeds regret's ripe bloom and brooding's bachelor morbidity. Cities avail with parties, to equip sex with chance meeting mates on romantic intoxication's exalted summit or drunken lust's permissiveness while the slumbering censor's strict forbidding is sneakily eased and furtively broken. I heed nature to watchfully wait, to let no opportunity slip.

Then you emulate my fate?

May those gods permit, whose blessing has been shed on you. A party's chance, and girls outcrowding the men.

Not to be. There's no repeating. Hope died, with the first loss, for all second tries: endeavor as you may in the desperate pride of futility.

Morose remorse spreads melancholy's solitary gloom. Woe on society, that natural countryside was never abolished to keep the city safely undistracted from the party's primary necessity as a marriage bureau or harvester of affairs sprung from planted roots on the spot. May unbroken scenery be cursed: A country scene, wrung from serenity, is worse by far than the city party's seeds of obscenity. A lesson later learned than application may remedy.

Peace. Next life may be a party, from beginning to end.

If so, my death will happily prepare it: I'm willing to go.

Then on the note of hope, may your suicide succeed.

Hell's a city, in lust's eternal greed. A fire warmed by merry spirits; a party of almost all girls, whose centrally affixed heaven is me, godlike, revolving among them, great of choice. Dreams of a better afterworld. Utopian consolation.

Go ahead. I've done well here. Try *your* chances, elsewhere.

BETWEEN PARTIES

The last party I went to was lots of fun. There were plenty of kinds of drinks to choose from, and enough food to stuff a starving army. And there were more men than women. Which was good for me, being a woman myself. I was at loose ends for want of a steady boyfriend, so I was sort of "on the make." I was prepared to be flirted with and to flirt back to fan two flames into one. I wasn't going to deprive myself of fun, intending fully to make a conquest. I was in that "dangerous mood." I would take the high romantic risk. Where would it lead? Up the primrose path? Or down into Sindale? The chance would be taken.

I arrived with already lots of guests there. I was being stared at right away, for they were mostly men and I looked just simply ravishing, at first glance, and later too. I couldn't even now *begin* to describe the clothing I wore! It was frilly feminine, and clinging. I looked adorably helpless. Men would come flocking to my distress, to rescue me—from each other! They would knock each other down, for the privilege. Let them have a battle-royal for me. Aren't I worth their blood, their pelts and bruises? Ah, how I'm going to bask in their competitive attention! But maybe in the end—*I'll* have the scars!

I hope I don't fall in love with the one who wins me. However, I might. The others have all abandoned the contest and left the field to him. They saw how I was involuntarily heeding him, to the exclusion of them. I kept staring at him. He won me over, with great eyes.

Other women were the consolation prizes for the men who lost me to my conquering hero—whose name is Lou, commonplacely enough; but now "Lou"—the name—is garlanded over with flowery bouquets, laurel wreaths, and other romantic effects borrowed from botany, that most ancient of all natural sciences.

Lou just dashingly plucked me. I no more could resist him, than a starving bird can resist a juicy worm. To this party came I exulting with my buoyantly conquering mood: and I wound up enslaved. What will Lou do with me? He takes me home, that's what.

"Home" means his, not mine. Now he's going to seduce me. I can feel it coming. Already, he's at my dress.

His eyes have thick lashes, with brows of villain-sophistication. His hand is feeling me all up. I'm getting moist with non-resistance. I'm in his power, while slowly I'm being enveloped. I had lots to drink, too. I'm loose, I'm relaxed, I'm drunk, I'm in love. I'm being overwhelmed, Lou is on me, with nothing on. Love has come out as sex.

I'm asleep. So is he. Under the sheets and blankets, we have nothing on. We've been intimate. But he's a mysterious stranger. What do I remember about him? He's in some sort of profession. But it's a blur, anything more specific than that.

I get up, to examine his apartment, peep at envelopes addressed to him or other telltale little documents lying about. What can I find out?

But I'm hung over from the night before. I'm in a kind of waking fog.

I discover nothing. I can't focus. I return to the bedroom. He's out of bed, in the bathroom. Now he comes out, approaching me. His eyes are at me. I'm helpless. I melt, before his advance. Now I'm softly within his grip. We're back on bed, now. We're more aware, this time—or *I* am, anyway. He's at me again, we're intimate. I just shrivel up, at his beck.

He's making breakfast for me. It's a Sunday morning, last night was the party, where I met him. But who is this "Lou"? And are his intentions honorably permanent for me? I'm growing toward middle age, and have yet even once to be married. What's Lou's occupation? I don't even care what, if only I could call him a husband soon. *That* could be his occupation: occupied with me. I would be his concern. I'd keep him busy, busy caring for me, investing in me. I'd be a going concern, for him— a testing enterprise. I speak over the breakfast table. He doesn't reply, and tells me put on all my outer clothing and leave his apartment. I offer to dictate my phone number to him, he doesn't reply, I write my phone number on a piece of paper, I hand him the paper, he hands it back without looking, he's opening the door, sort of edging me out, I ask him when could I see him again, he shrugs and kind of shoves me out, the door is now shut, I press the doorbell, I press it hundreds of times, and not once does the door get opened, I'm out here weeping, the party was a lot of fun last night, lots to drink and all that. I felt seductive before and after entering, now it's morning and I'm abandoned. I'm getting too old for this. I want security, an orderly household, a stable husband. This idea wouldn't seem to appeal to Lou, in regard to me. I'll forget him, that'll be easy. I only met him last night. I have Sunday before me. I'll phone friends up, I don't want to be alone. It's scary to be alone, right now.

I'm in a street public phone booth near Lou's apartment house. I make a phone call, but wake up my friend, who seems annoyed and tells me to phone back later. Lots of people would be sleeping late on Sunday morning. I keep on looking through the window of the phone box toward Lou's building, in case he ever emerges. Others do, from other apartments; but no Lou. Oh, forget Lou. What a mood I was in when I entered the party! I was confidently radiating. Among others, it attracted Lou. Too bad some *other* man didn't win me. I might be a lot happier, now.

Why am I still here in the phone booth waiting? Why for Lou?, he already rejected me. Do I hope for better treatment, or do I want more punishment? The sun is out, it's a nice day.

I'll take a walk, it's near the park. Then I'll phone up my friends again: with better results, this time.

I straggle away from the booth, I give up. To hell with Lou. Who could I have met and gotten nicely involved with to a better outcome, had not Lou won me over with his eyes and manner? I could be *so* much happier. I'll be much more prudent, next party. I was just an impulsive fool, and drank too much. Then I was a pushover, for Lou. And then he pushed me over. I'm determined, never again. I can't take much of this any more. I'm getting too old, I need to settle down. Lou was just a brief fate. No more Lou. I want real love, next time.

I like this walk. It's leading me somewhere. The day is lovely. The park smells fresh. Oh, I feel romantic!

But it could get me in trouble, feeling romantic. I better watch out and not be such a sucker. I fell too easy—to the wrong chap. I'll know *much* better. I already knew better, but it happened anyway. I haven't just been born. I've been around. But I'm still hopeful. Too naive. No more Lou's, for me.

Who? Who instead? Who? And where is he? Where? And when? When?

It will be. I can virtually see it. I know it.

I know it, but when will I confirm it? So it officially will happen? Will take place? Will come to pass. To be. Actually be. A lovely man, for me. Lovely, and enduring. To love me, always.

Already, I can taste him. I can feel him. He's so real. But why doesn't he materialize?

I haven't met him yet! But there's a party, I'll go to it, there he'll be, it's next week, Friday night, I'll wait for then. It's only Sunday yet. I have lots of time.

A CALCULATED BUT MISFIRED FRIENDSHIP (BASED ON A PROFESSION. BUT HEALTH INTERVENED. IT CAME BETWEEN US.)

I met a doctor socially at a party by accidentally being introduced to him during a drinking confusion.

Then he and I were talking, talking, and talking, which is what people mostly do at parties because drinking lubricates the tongue and after all the occasion is deliberately social.

He grew to like me, I liked him, already we had become friends and we had only just met. I realized I could take advantage of him. (Which is what friendship is for, mostly.) I could get cured, for he was a doctor.

He had been through medical school at considerable expense. He had served his term of internship for many fruitful years of exacting toil, of prolonged service. And for the last few years he had set up practice on his own and was earning a respectable living case after case of curing people. As I had become his friend, I could be his patient free.

But what could he cure me of? I was free of disease, and surgery would be an unnecessary waste. So how could I avail myself of his friendship, he being a doctor? I'd have to *make* myself ill so that he could have something to cure. Perhaps a self-inflicted wound, inflicted on myself, would I try to inflict. Or I could incur a hypochondriacal sickness which would enlist his free services as my special medical friend.

But alas, the timing was bad, for just at that time, ironically, I was in perfect health. My body was simply *smoldering* with health. Health was leaking out of me, in all directions.

But the more it leaked out, the more I was resupplied with it, until my body was just *oozing* with health, like an indomitable fortress.

What good is a doctor friend in a situation like *that*? All those years painstakingly studying in medical school, the infinitely laborious casework as an intern at the clinic, and his profitable recent years as an upstanding and practicing doctor, a pillar of the community—were now an outstanding *waste*, so far as I was concerned. And all I cared about was how *I* was concerned. That was the way I practiced friendship—I *gave* of myself, and deeply.

The friendship went on, for *years*. And I simply stayed healthy. Little did he, in his simplicity, realize how much money it had already cost me in free doctor bills not to have been ill. He was too friendly to understand. As far as I was concerned, he was costing me plenty a year. Then, I developed a common cold. My friend treated it so inexpensively it wasn't worth my trouble.

Therefore, think twice, before making friends with someone and getting so deep in frustration like I did: I, who had speculated on bad health, reckoned wrong, and was losing so much imaginary money each year on behalf of a "pure" friendship. Next time, a worthier investment. A friend to *really* depend on.

A PROGRESSIVELY PERFECT PARTY

"Oh how sensationally elegant," claimed the person for whom a party always at least had the consolation of being an occasion. The person to whom this was confided frowned with a genteel smirk. Scotch in considerable quantity was being consumed.

Persons of either sex in a stunning array of interestingness kept repeatedly "arriving". Rooms flowed in their swaying circuits. Half romantically, the lamps were kindled with dimness.

Conversationally, an extremely varied versatility of vocalism on all sides assaulted the defenseless ears. Strips of wit were sliced with other odd patterns of speech. Articulateness asserted the total gamut within its range.

There were some indeed quite personal scenes. On the open exchange of mobile permissiveness, a market of contacts between freshly met men and women was to an exceeding degree active in every alive sense of vitality. Hardly veiled flirtations hinted, not nearly so vaguely, at the rich emotional promise of romance. By the clothing they did not seem to be wearing, some women postured a sensuous brand of beauty. The animals of men's eyes admired them with frank astonishment.

Between fractured particles of group-shifts, the figure of an attentive host could be spotted, engaged in a conversation imperiled by distractions lurking nearby with every opportunity. A female "helper" of his (said to be his "steady") replenished tables laden with bowls of onion mixture and tasty, crunchy cheese crackers. Of course, on other tables an adult assortment of alcoholic beverages was ample to combat socially instilled thirst of inhibition-removed guests. "A success!", said someone unseen behind a mass silhouette of heads. It was to the party, obviously, that his remark referred, and others assented with nods or murmurs indicative of gratification in the stance of human sociality. The comment was soon relayed to the host, who most pardonably beamed in relief for the ardor of accomplishment.

One room was set aside (accessible from two entrances) for popular dances then in modern fashion, accompanied by the booming rhythms stamped out on a phonograph needle. This rampant music trumpeted a therapeutic sequence of release. Dancers were compressed, and groins pulverized tightly together.

Primal beats were in swing. Squirming practitioners of a ritualistic paganism abandoned their limbs to the glorious melody of lust.

One room, with panting red tonality, was sinisterly dark to thump up the erotic pulse. In corners of disarray, couples sprawled in positions according to acceptable procedure of semi-public orthodoxy in the casual art of indecency. Like snakes, their bodies first would writhe, then fall. (This party's guest-list was confined to those who professed a liberal persuasion in codes of debatably moral conduct. Prudes were so far out of fashion, the times had left them to the ludicrous and eccentric forms of modest decorum. Ridicule would shame them into the more vogue-ish norms of amorality, short of the genuinely scandalous, Shock was too extremist for the revised protocols of good taste.)

Some gate crashers tried to bluff admission on pretenses of having been invited by "a friend", but they were repulsed by an alerted host; his select party thus preserving its virginity of exclusiveness. The guests appreciated this flatteringly inferred appraisal of their status. Their intimacy squeezed itself closer. They cosily kept in swing, thrilling to the shared smugness of their limited "belonging".

Alcoholically, a few inebriates staggered with reduced control of conscious faculties. They were however inoffensive, so that the party still boiled over with the big power in its brilliance. A party that robust could not be disintegrated from within by a scattered assemblage of those whose participation was stilted in drunken stupor. The hour was advanced far past midnight. No one even *wanted* to leave. A union in glitter held them rhapsodically there.

THE DULLEST PARTY IMAGINABLE

(A Party So Dull, You Couldn't Imagine How Dull It Was. Too Boring, Really, To Tell Of. Yet, Be Told, You Dull Reader.)

Probably, without stretching hyperbole into exaggeration, it was—second to none—positively the dullest party that the earth had ever known in the whole history of living matter—or at least since there were enough people on earth to constitute the quorum or minimal number to assemble an official party into its collective organic being, (Which may first have happened in the dim recesses of prehistory's antique dawn, in the early annals far back in the primitive era of oral grunts which characterized the profound illiteracy of those remote times.)

Meanwhile, back to this dullest party ever: at which it was my misfortune to be drearily in attendance.

It was so dull, the guests were sitting or standing around with a moping look of emotionless (unless boredom qualifies as an emotional category) vacancy of sheer nullity, or numbness; looking like life doing an amateur imitation of death's unquick state.

The guests stirred their mental faculties in wonderment to puzzle out what could be done to liven up this party: which, at the moment, seemed to be basking in its own funeral stew, like a corpse perspiring on an unnecessarily hot day, thus smelling up his ill-fitting shroud in a sweltering casket whose inexpensive wood was warping its way into a rotten advancement of chemical decomposition in a wooden parallel of corresponding rot to the decay itself of its sweat-drenched resident corpse under the stifling shroud on a stultifyingly humid afternoon unfit equally for life or post-life, in whatever state.

What could bring this party to life? The guests could barely ponder this point, since the weariness of dull lassitude kept retarding their thought faculties to an arrested state that dimly held Illumination in a blindfolded and gagged condition of abject captivity, under the wardenship of that shapeless creature, Dullness.

To say—or state—that this was a dull party, would be to commit an understatement so unfunny that even as an understatement it takes on the dullness of the party thus described.

Let's just say it was a dull party—and leave it at that. Why embellish a point thus simply declared in a bald, factual directness blandly unadorned in the bold courage of its own descriptive dullness?

It's academic to debate whether this party was more boring than dull, or more dull than boring. Why try? Let's compromise by saying that the party's boringness and the same party's dullness were each parties to the same thing. Anything further along these lines would aspire to the monotony of hairsplitting—a useless and tedious scruple which the case couldn't possibly justify, under the dead weight of its unenlightening content.

As a subject, the party—or the dullness thereof—or both—has already long begun to pall.

Since the party was (to put it mildly) without interest, why dwell on it, why prolong an unrewarding discussion—or reiteration—of its so dull a dullness as not even to have the strength to be at least well-nigh insufferable?

The dullness was so dull, it lacked the guts even to annoy the bored guests—who remained stupefied, listless, lifeless, apathetic, languid, and just barely conscious while yet unblessed by the merciful oblivion that sleep would afford, as a relief or way-out in retirement from the thick gauze of boring uniform dullness that spread over the party's atmosphere in uneventful evenness of lack-texture.

"To liven up this party," said Betsy (who was no more nor no less a guest than all her colleague guests stuck equally in this miserable excuse for a party), "Let's introduce a game."

This hopeful suggestion failed to rally her flagging co-guests to even the bottom rung of enthusiasm's towering ladder.

Pluckily, undiscouraged, Betsy next proposed the following potentially constructive suggestion: "Does anyone know any magic tricks?"

The response—if any—was lost in the neutral pall of silence that densely "united" the zombie assemblage of the lifeless gathering.

Persistently, Betsy struck another approach: "Would anyone like to give a reading or recital from his or her writing, providing he or she has his or her manuscript here handy?"

What greeted this couldn't even be said to resemble even a groan, or a moan. Stupefied dullness reigned in grim negation, massively defended behind an unassailable fortress by the implacable forces of unhearing inarticulateness.

"Dull?" Such a word doesn't even *begin* to fully describe, in any complete way, the absolute levelled-down dullness that held this party in its gripping sway in a vice-like grip that choked the arterial breath from the smothered multiple cadaver that constituted what remained (humanly speaking) of this so-called feeble excuse for a party.

"Party"? It was too dull to be one.

"Non-party"? That, at least, would come closer to describing this altogether too dreary affair.

Betsy wouldn't give up. Once she had an idea in her head, she'd beat it to death before, as a last resort, admitting failure or defeat. Undaunted, she cried, "Shame on you, my fellow guests! This party simply hasn't 'taken off.' None of you has come boldly forward to don the mantle and assume the role as self-proclaimed 'life of the party.'"

"We've all just sullenly stood by, while this non-starting party droops in collapse—or rather, in non-collapse, lacking even something to collapse *from*: a comparatively full preceding phase of itself.

"This party is moribund. Its 'demise' is a misnomer, since it never once attained any life from which such life's demise would then, in effect, succeed.

"Jointly, it's all our faults, in group nonresponsibility, that this party hasn't even earned the dignity to be entitled to be *called* a party, so partyless has this somber lump of a lifeless congregation remained from its unpromising start up to—or down to—this passing empty moment masquerading nominally as 'the present.' Temporality has vanished, in the inconsequentiality of this joint creature we're all components of. It's *been* nowhere, *gone* nowhere, and *is* nowhere. It's a nonentity—in which we each partake, as a vital cell.

"I won't stand by helpless while this party—in front of our very eyes—continues not taking place."

Betsy's harangue grew shrill. Her diatribe raged in the fury of her impassioned solitary stand, her one-woman crusade against the collective glaze of emptiness sunk in its own apathy and vacantly not caring.

Again, she stormed and ranted in the violence of her caring plea, in the fervor of her committed cause, to move the mass from its massive slough of immobility, from its primeval ooze in the lumbering slumber of its own slime, bestially slow to the barely beating pulse of its passivity:

"Listen to me, folks. Bestir your senseless dormancy, and attend me thus:

"This, folks, is a *party*—or is *supposed* to be.

"To the degree that it's not—and it sure isn't—it's laughable.

"I implore you—let's get this party going: let's haul it off the ground, prop it on its vertical, pump some air into it, flail it into breathing, punch some life into it, heave it into the semblance of even the rudiments of the first stirrings of animation, to break its inert impasse and finally get rolling.

"What is, potentially, this party's life? It's the sum of all of *us*—that's right, *us*. Meaning *you*; me too.

"The people of a nation are not necessarily the government that purports to represent them. But the people of a party, in total, constitute the party itself. Well . . ." (a pause for emphasis) " . . . that's our cue, folks.

"*We—we*'re the life of the party. It's in *our* hands—collectively.

"Then what are we waiting for? Let's go, gang!"

Her shout pierced the airless air, like a dummy slug shot—a dud of a thud—from a child's toy pistol. Meant to activate those sluggish non-listeners, it merely merged with the wall of indifference that facelessly had formed there.

But Betsy wouldn't be put off. The "sting" of this "rebuff" merely clenched her resolve rousing and stirred to the fierce acceptance of a "challenge" to which in fiery mettle she was determined—against all combative odds—relentlessly to rise with the apostle's zeal of a strict crusade to be culminated with conquest's crown in routing triumph over the phantom non-assailants mossed in the apathetic web spun in the odorless stench of torpor's malignant growth in a self-produced fungus-colony nest that breeds the pestilence of drowsy indifference from the pus-fertilized home-grown plant of a mass drug that attacks a party crowd with irresistible infection and group con-tamination on the slow, sure, plodding wings of conformity's lifeless contagion dedicated to spoil any would-be party with the scorpion's bite of the flapless spirit of negation.

Such an adversary Betsy elects to fight. She alone wasn't bit-ten by the dreary-bug; she alone is immune to this all-sweeping blasé-germ, to whose spell or thrall all the other guests have unfightingly succumbed in the doped chamber of this enchant-ment.

Again, she cajoles, like a battering ram energized by a built-in steam dynamo:

"Who'll show the first promptings of life, in shaking off ina-nition's lumpish paralysis? I've just put dance music on the record player—hear it blare. Can you feel pulsing its irresistible rhythm? Then move your limbs—dance!"

The music record moved in its grooves, automatically, mechanically—but with no enlivening effect on the deadheads whose bodies alone—barely—were in attendance in the apartment rooms where, that night, a party had been scheduled, for which occasion all these guests had arrived. They were physically there. But somehow, something was lacking. The party lacked "verve." It lacked a certain intangible "something." In fact, it lacked more than that: it lacked, foremost, even the element of tangibility. In its own spiritual void, this "social gathering" was hushed—ready to coil? To spring? No. To waste. To evaporate. To become all the nothing it seems endlessly to promise, during its long practice period of no spark, no sparkle, no contact, no communication, no recognition, no encounter; no sign of life among people—for which normally a party is definitionally functioned.

Betsy is admonishing the crowd; but to the crowd her roars seem like indistinguishable dronings that blend in with the prevailing nothingness motif.

But who lives there in the apartment? The host and hostess do. But who can tell them apart from all the lumpen guesthood? No-one, not even maybe the hosts themselves. Consciousness isn't exactly a commodity in abundance, right now, here.

Only one individual stands out, from this generalized human stupefaction vacuum: Betsy. In her one-woman campaign to undeaden this dreary wasteland of mindless empty forms all crowded here in dense idle dunce-ity, she vigorously rails to the gathered multitude against the boredom they seem effortlessly to generate in superfluous magnitudes of abundance. Nothing doing. In uniform dullness, Betsy's non-audience dimly fails to respond.

Dullness has won out, this evening. Even Betsy's force of rhetoric fails—quite dismally—to offset, or even challenge, the established, set, rooted, hardened, all-sweeping dominion of rule-by-dullness. It's settled, impervious, like mineral gravity weighing leadenly on low-slung earth.

Betsy screeches on—unheard, into the endless party. The host and hostess are mingled indistinguishably in the overall guest corps. Guests, by now, can't tell each other apart. They're melted, welded, into one mass-clutter, scattered throughout the apartment rooms in separate body segments or clung clusters of humankind in its unworthiness aspects.

No positive evil, badness, damage, or harm has been done, beyond dullness for its own sake: sustained even beyond monotony, self-contained in the monstrous boredom that's too bored even to discern itself.

Drone on, Betsy. The night lengthens. As yet, no-one has left. Newcomers have been arriving, all this while, to glut the boredom bulk in heaped-on hordes and squads of sameness-packed reinforcement.

"Wake up! You indolent slugs! You're swelling boredom's saturation ratio to unheard-of degrees far beyond the monotonous equilibrium smack-level in the central balance of the endless core—in a perpetually self-replenishing cycle—of dullness feeding on its own durable dullness self."

Thus screamed Betsy. No-one, exactly, was thrilled.

THE TWO BEST-MANNERED GENTLEMEN, UNFORGETTABLY, MEET.

There were two men of impeccable manners: extremely well bred: Jonathan, and Ikano (whose ancestors were Japanese). However, they never met. This was remedied by a social woman who knew them both. She invited them both to the same dinner party. They were so polite, they arrived (with their respective wives) not too early, not too late. Some guests sided with Jonathan as the world's most well-mannered gentlemen, while others championed Ikano for that supreme title. Some backers from the opposed camps even placed wagers on the contest. But was it to be a contest? The essence of good manners was in refraining from competition. Jonathan courteously refused to compete; so did Ikano: And their manners were never so brilliant, so dazzling to behold, as just then, in their courteous mutuality's standoff stalemate. Breeding told, in this instance. And those uncouth enough to wish for the discord of gentlemen were put to quiet shame, by so dignified a concord.

Manners oft proclaim the man. Then loudly heralded are gentle Jonathan and superb Ikano, by what they do, or refrain from doing. The dinner party was a revelation. It was graced by the nicest prizes of civilization: superb Jonathan, gentle Ikano. They're blessed here on the land of earth. Later they'll honor heaven, and flatter all angelic hosts in such celestial realm, with their cultivated adaptability to place and protocol, providing the circumstance with delicate, unbombastic attentions that smooth over awkward ruffles and place their fellow creatures in a serene and esteemed composure. Manners are gifts, in the finest sense. Jonathan and Ikano *are* gifts—they're bestowed generously, on us.

We accept them gratefully. We're worthy of them, by taking them for our models. Let conduct soothe the travail of others, and provide sweet delight. Let's increase the general wealth. For we partake, too.

SPIRITS RISING ABOVE WATER LEVEL

Try to keep your head above water . . .

It's *high* above water.

High how?

On spirits.

But do water and alcohol mix?

In *my* heady atmosphere, yes. I'm so drunk, I'm sober drunk.

Can those extremes meet?

In *my* heady atmosphere, yes.

FIRST CAME WATER

What a waste, that water should be so wet! I think wetness is a superfluous property, that makes water unnecessarily redundant. Therefore water should sacrifice wetness (being wet enough), and donate its essentially surplus excess of property to painfully dry things, like barren rocks, thirsty plants, desolate deserts, and decaying wood. But this would be socialism, and would horrify the capital out of my American soul. So I guess inequality has its place, if free enterprise is to endure, and so let water maintain its monotony—I mean monopoly—on liquid, fluid wetness—or even on still wetness, in a stagnant pool or quiet ocean, if it so chooses. *Laissez faire* is my motto, and if water owns a vast wealth of wet—has invested its soul in wet, and floated liquid stocks in it, and commands a bond with it, so that the quality is inexhaustible by quantity—then let it be. If survival makes the fittest, then, by the law of the jungle—but preferably that of the ocean—the rivers and lakes of the world ought to acknowledge water. And when it rains, that's still further evidence. What is one to do?—defy God? No, deify Him, or we'll be all wet. So if my theory holds water, and slakes the thirst of truth, then no use crying vain tears (artificial water, and not the real thing itself, but a salted man-made product, synthetically caused by grief), but let's base our life on water, and all praise it, the good basic element that rounds out the addition of our life, a fertile force opposed to sterility; let's join in the swim, laud our origin, unite, and say, "God bless the water!" Once having said that, we're free to keep out of the rain: *if* there's rain, which is not always guaranteed, especially when the weather is good.

Good old water. However, I prefer alcohol. Only the dead can get drunk on water, if they've drowned in it. I prefer to keep my feet dry, and my tongue wet, and intoxicate my inward spirits with an outward addition to the beverages of fire—whisky, for instance. Without water, thank you. Perhaps with ice. But here's hoping that the ice doesn't melt, not until emptiness has removed the contents of my glass, so that staggering, I yell: "Holy water! Baptize me in it!" and collapse, a happy man, solid, formed of earth. Hurray. With tons of water in me, the fire of my spirits tinted and tainted and taunted by the universal life-giver. Three cheers for water. When I stand up, I'll know what I'm saying, but meanwhile, I'm drunk on life, and drowning in all that blesses. What does air mean, when water suffices? Again, I'm a fish, and reverse evolution. I'll swim back to the paramoeba, and declare my first cell, and be pre-born. With all of destiny before me, man not even conceived, and God a beardless youth, surviving His adolescence, creating the future with some clay, to which He sprinkles the addition of water, to modify, perhaps to purify, as the unformed monsters clash in His brain, the creatures fertilized to earth, born of the spray. Ah, the sands of time, the beach of spawned activity, and always the tides moving in. Thank you, God. I have enough water. The water is fine. That's quite enough. No more, thank you. Now it's too much, and my poor breath is gone. Down I'm under, in this kingdom of wet, my soul dry. And now, only forever remains. Dry, but preserved. No more liquid fury, the shifting shapes. Eternity's monument, out of the sea. Where no ship dwells, no fins or gills exist, but simply, without time, something dry and breathless, a deep container, filled with emptiness, that spills over. Beyond the brim, an everlasting fountain. Or a well, holding to the middle of the earth, from which a great nothing is drawn, pumped, yielded, a glory renewed in its birth, always but never the same, to which water and earth were doubly joined, born to be dead simultaneously. What a unity. Where wet and dry, death and life, nothing and all, can't be separate, and have their great unification. Then what can divide us? How can we be alone? All this, everything, and nothing.

And nothing being so abundant, it contains everything. Surely, what more is needed? Water can slench the thirst, anything can do anything, and great Nothing contains all. The sea, let us go to the everlasting sea. And see our simple beginning.

THE ORIGINAL UNDILUTED PURITY OF ICE CUBES IMMERSED IN AN ALCOHOLIC BEVERAGE. AN ANTI-MELTING PLEA

If you wait too long, your ice cubes will melt and dilute your "pure" drink. When they're still solid ice and just put into the glass, the cubes *aid* the purity of the alcohol in it. Then, gradual deterioration, dilution, dissolution of purity. Then, you have a watered-down drink. A violation of the true alcoholic content.

So *time* is important, in this as well as in other cases. Hurry up and quickly finish your drink before the ice cubes have a chance to melt: while they're solidly entire, unchipped-away at by the chemical action of time and the liquid they're immersed in. They're pure when just issued straight out of the freezing compartment of the refrigerator. Please defend their purity, and that of the liquid they're immersed in, by drinking up, quick. Then the refill, and get purely drunk. This is the "swill" system, of swift drinking. Its dangerous excess lead to stages of alcoholism, the addictive and chronically drunk. Avoid that, be moderate. But keep the ice cubes pre-meltedly in their original big size. Don't let them lessen. That's the lesson, and let's drink to it.

Bottoms up, or it's too late. Hurry, hurry, the world won't wait.

I HAVE AN EERIE FEELING THAT WHAT I'M JUST GOING THROUGH WAS FOREORDAINED AND WAS HAPPENING TO THE WHOLE RACE ALL THE TIME BEFORE I GOT HERE—AND WHEN I PASS IT ON, IT'LL BE JUST AS COMMON. WHAT'S IT ALL BEING REHEARSED FOR—A SHOWDOWN?

(Scene: A bar. Two strangers meeting on the stools by the counter.)

Here we are at a bar, so I suppose we must drink. It's more fun doing it together, so whatever your name is, let's introduce each other, and at these adjoining stools we can settle down, foot on the brass rail below, and order and drink. Do you have a *standard* tale of woe? If so, get it over with, rid your chest of what you often tell, so we can get down to what we're really thinking *now*.

You've set us up to be in a bar situation.

But that's where we are in *fact*.

But you've made it so that I can think only of a typical bar situation and wonder if we're conforming to it.

A few drinks will rid you of this self-conscious addiction to comparing the present with a stereotype image of its *Absolute* atmosphere, the archetype for anyone in modern times being in a bar in this country in the biggest city where you're so lost that if you're in trouble with loneliness at night you repair to a bar to fit yourself for drunken companionship or a drunken verbal bout short of a brawl. Contemporary fiction is full of scenes like this.

I've been through so many before, in person, and vicariously through the relatings of others who have, and scenes like this are stamped on television, and are a stock plot chorus that readers of manly adventure stories will recognize, hard-boiled types often frequent the bar, or those down on their luck or in despair. Movies and magazines have innumerably depicted just as it is now for us. I feel I'm being dreamt by a collective myth.

But don't you trust that between us we'll make it all somehow different?, in our very special case of being at *this moment*, not anytime else, *here* of all bars, not any other bar. This is a plastic situation just *made* for our self-creating. It's like a farmer every day for sixty years being on his same modest acres working—each new day is for itself, if the farmer is alive at the moment to all the differences. It depends on *us*, not to be slaves to the cumulative typicalness of two men being in a bar on such a night of such a big modern city. We won't succumb, will we?, to this *seeming* like a stock situation? We have it in our power to make it real and unique for ourselves tonight—so that in future years, memory will praise this creative event. We're not characters, because we're in *life*.

The way you define our possibilities of removing ourselves from the stereotype, and encourage our confidence to transcend it—your analysis is *itself* a stereotype of existential contemporary philosophy. I've heard it all before—hearing you deny it all. I think we're both locked in a fiction plot, and can't get out. Unfortunately, the author or playwright of us is drearily unoriginal, so that neither you nor I can be lifted outside our being wooden characters of flat and instant recognizability for the reader's lazy ease, to fill a typical bar scene that's going nowhere. We're just putting in time here. We're drinking and rambling. The background is as it should be. A hackneyed preconception by a collection of tradition-bound mediocre unoriginals has fixed us to our insipid predicament of wondering whether this is real, or whether we are, and what it's all leading to. I'm bored, like the modern man *should* be.

I beg to differ. A cliché is only if you permit it to be. It's true that the reiterated contemporary themes are man's alienation, man's identity, man's existence, men's interrelatedness, and the human bond of a common tragedy. What do you think this bar is *for*? We're here to discuss it all again.

I'm tired of the same old thing. I want to be surprised by an experience in outer space.

There are drugs to administer to such desperation, that extend consciousness into extraordinary hallucination. Or even the old-fashioned method of getting drunk will induce some illusions or delusions that remove the stale flatness from our insipid rut of experience. Are you getting half-drunk by now? Isn't your mind glowing into change?

Yes, and it looks like you too. I'm beginning to feel slightly more wonderful. Even a floating lust is starting to get re-aroused. Is there a late party we can go to when we finish these drinks, where maybe some girls are looking for us? It's always an exciting change of state to get hot with a new girl. We can enter into romantic situations: hackneyed, just like this one.

To remove ourselves from a trite bar atmosphere in a typical enormous American city, and, with our author's permission, to have the luck of fooling around with some pretty, new girls (not here, where they're all escorted or only ugly barflies and widow-like divorcees, but somewhere to change our environment), for us to get into an unexpected, exciting, marvelous—but equally trite, just as preordained—eroticoromantic heaven in absorption with girls we like and who like us? That's been in the movies before, in the theatre, on television, on radio, in books with hard covers and soft covers, and in all periodical pulp. The Greeks made nothing new under the sun. There are recurring cycles of repeating—that's what *Finnegans Wake* is about, if you can understand it. (Written by the self-exiled Irish Joyce.) Can we expect nothing of life, then, than one surprising cliché after another? The question was asked long ago: "What are we here for?" Its relevance is still pertinent, don't you think?, to the site and clime of our modern time? The unreasoned echo of an old and clinging rhyme.

History had millions of men like us, but most of them are dead. They all felt unique—when they weren't feeling dull. What's *our* importance in the generational Space of all Time?

That's a big question. I'm not metaphysical enough to answer it.

Then finish your drink, and let's go to this party I know. When a man is lonely, the delight of meeting girls is especially acute—it has a wild intensity, like fate or instinct. *(They raise themselves from bar stools.)* But wait—hasn't this whole scene been re-enacted before?: What we've just said, where we've been, and where we're off now to go to? We're about to be in transition from the bar to a setting with girls in it who we hope will be available—and who promise to be desirable, though in our state that wouldn't take much. It's all been gone through before. Who by? Us?

And enough others for this to be a racial inheritance, the legendary human memory applying itself to this moment of our passing in motion—us, from this bar, to somewhere else. It's familiar to something similar—but what?

We're acting small roles that have always been acted, by previous actors, and other actors elsewhere, and by the nonentities of tomorrow's stage. We feel like every man who ever existed—even the farm-bound man who never stepped in a bar. All men before us felt sexual anticipation after drinking a little too much, and were about to be going off on the girl chase. That's a tableau frozen on a Greek vase and fixed to all imitations of life, arrested by sufficient repetition. We're going through this same phase of immortality—with just the classical touch to assure our universality. It's the good old style, that never fails. It does me proud. I'm given my humble place—and it's *great*! Now, every step I make is bound to be in the authoritative stride of all mankind's generation from cell up through explosive species, and with that backing I pace my triumph!

You don't sound so lonely as you did earlier.

No, all that is cured now. I'm from an all-inclusive lineage! All men who ever were, are acting in me now. Through me, can you hear their undead striding?

That's formidable support you're given—high-stepping in their transferable but unworn-out shoes. You have every reason behind you, for confidence in doing what you're about to do. The rhythm of precedence is so uninhibiting! When within tradition, we're suddenly so decisive!—our acts are manly, undisputable, Godlike! A sporting comparison comes now to mind: It's like kicking a football with all history's wind at your back—the ball sails in a high and unending arc. There's a bracing blast of inevitability to give superhumanity to our feat. Take *us*, about to leave this bar, to pursue some yet unknown skirts—the homeliest of illustrations, vulgarly close to commonplace. What we're up to isn't new—but its age is our strength. Instinct's very lack of originality, its inflexibility of non-imagination, is a weighty force of power impelling motivation's bolt in motion. What momentum we've been given! It's terrific, to be in such step. *(Chants a couplet:)*

> We'll get those girls, who don't know it yet.
> It's determined they're ours, no need to bet!

(Back to "normal" talking:) This bar has seen us enough. Time to swagger from it. *(Leaving bar stools, they head resolutely for exit:)* We stagger to do what's been done so much, who knows if *we're* doing it, or just some other men? Like the role of Hamlet that doesn't care who plays it? Or the striding Achilles that's still belting our rhythm along? Now I feel in *touch*. What act I do, is the whole Act at once! *(They pause before exit. More hesitantly:)* Or am I taking too much on myself? Is my grandeur borrowed from the whole, of which I shrink to a minor part, selfishly inebriated with insignificance? I've taken legends of history and literature, those open public documents, and put in my private

claim. This invincibility I've been assuming—is an invisibility? Are those girls assuredly ours tonight?—who we've drunkenly not met yet? Doubt comes rippling in, and our inherited certainty is a ripped-apart document not notarized in current.

Why this lapse in hope? We're playing the *confident* man's role.

Behind us are sagas of accident and downright failure, the abundant falling short of all men—especially those built in *my* mold: The stumbling ones who were tripped up in their comical flop to defeat—and were grandiosed to call their plight tragic, whose flight was abortive with their folly. I contritely shrink back, with a palling and futile heart. The blood has fled from me. Will *you* instill new courage in us, with the false booming of rationalization? An undaunted spirit has flown somewhere else; and my soul has burst in my face, making me a laughing stock—or stock character. How do *you* take stock, of this abrupt farce? Drink is not to be trusted—it *flows* too much, and leads us to no solid reasoning when its fluid state prompts a fluent babble.

Elusive grace has been snatched from our grasp. We can now pathetically cower, who had been one beat away from standing fast in all rhythms! A prize slipped away, that we barely clutched. What?

You're not bolstering us. We're *both* of sagging strength. Our shareable lapse has us doomed.

I had depended on *your* robust shape, to transfuse my hope anew. Instead, I'm infected by your somber cast. How did our aspiration reach its pang of decline, at once? We were boldly bent on conquest: the sap had been spinning; it met a reversed turn, and—by alarm—we're vanquished. We're twisted off the party. Those girls can never be retrieved. We haven't left the bar. We'll return to the drinking counter—our open spaces are still there. A sour venture is to be accounted for—why it took off and ended at the start. We'll drink a drop more than clarity can hold, and watch our heads pour over. We'll need a big ache to equate the frustrated hell of our spirit. That might clear up what problem there was no solution for: And were it drinkable, we'd drink that too. *(They return to take their place at their former bar stools, looking chastened and forlorn.)*

Have you figured out what happened to us? Earlier tonight we met here to drown sorrow. After a few drinks, we had gotten up to leave, in adventurous spirit, to join a late-blooming party. As we reached the transitional point, ready to put the bar behind and transfer ourselves to where the girls would be for whom anonymously we were in lust—we dropped back and lost our enterprise, sinking at the momentous surge that had lifted suspense up. We had been a masterful part of all ages, and the soul of man—from its conceiving evolution onward—was striding in the grace of our act. We had the borrowed power of an actor whose role is no less than the deified personification of man driven through God to a majestic perfection. Then the red-carpeted, regal-purpled earth was whisked away from under the winged storm of our feet—upturning our drive, and landing us back on bar stools. For an instant, there, an eternal moment of recognition was breathing epiphany in, with the mingled breath of archetype in our lungs transfixed to juggle time unstaled of its ever-divisive sequences. Man was forward in us as typical, and we joined his soul's Collective in the elect office of his one-voiced spokesman distilled from every tongue that ever gave language to the wind. The numbers we represented quite killed the mortality in us. Then the blessing was retracted, and we felt normal again.

We're in our more natural states. Were we presuming on the divine?

Drink and lust, and our companionship, had mingled a shock of power in us, and a grand rarity came down to fix our roles in it. Why couldn't we continue?

A glimpse flashed through, and then disappeared. We verged just short of the mystical.

Now just let's be typical guys drinking at a bar, to whom magic no more occurs than any other freak event. Let's take stock of this bar situation. Ages before have rehearsed this for us. We needn't think, any more. It's fit and meet that we be here, in a bar atmosphere loyal to its own stereotype, fixed and true to its first Absolute image in the archetype conception that set us up for all this. Here we are, and it's so real, that let art dare to imitate it without howling over into cliché. This is a literary event. Let's celebrate it, with the old usual toast, since it's almost closing time, and the morning is anxious to succeed night to see if it can do its old trick again.

What trick?

Conjure up a sun, from the same East.

That's just an illusion, if you consider it astronomically.

So are we, in our Act of real men acting as though they're acting out fictive roles. The world has been dramatized, and man has the star part as his own ham. Reality is dreaming in a theatre. The stage rolls over onto the audience. What a big act it all is!

We're here, only here. But I'm nostalgic for every here else. This is only this given night, late in the nineteen sixties, but for me it doesn't suffice, I seem to remember all the other times that men ever lived in: it's my *longing* to remember: but I don't *really* remember. I'm confined to this present time and place, and to my single self (and yours for company). But I'm nostalgic to group together, into one unit, every moment that every man ever experienced, as the joint property for which I'm the total heir. But no law court would honor my claim. They'd say I was only crazy. Of course, I *am* crazy. That's normal, given what man is. I can only be one where at the same time, so I know I'm one person. May this typical bar dissolve, so that other stock situations may move in—all at once, not successively. I'm in love with the Whole, but it doesn't requite me.

Is your clarity injured by being mildly drunk now? Your vision is so vast, that it couldn't be clear at all points. A *tiny* scope can be focused on, for illumination to devour, in the modesty of a single sight. *Your* view is very cloudy, for it heeds the far call of an illusion that blurs your flight to a diffusion of all the fantasy, a scattered shot of ranging disconnectedness that disperses as it spreads. That's why "God" is so vague: He's too many places at too many times. Man should concentrate on digesting one small bit, his local lot, and be content with it. It bespeaks his nature better, than to tumble off and stumble on, driven by the deceptive pranks of Impossibility, lured past his proper business into bungling invasions that territorially laugh at his illusion. You're consumed in a dream. The bar is about to close. The bartender is making signals at us. The other folks have left, and we've become loitered customers while the tables are being wiped off and the glasses are set awash in the sink and the bottles are being disposed of and there's a tinkling clearing up and the chairs are being put upside down on the clean tables so that the floor can be mopped without obstacles to obstruct. I think it's time we should leave. The bartender has an angry face. We're the sole ones left who don't work here, and a cop might peep in and be reported to, about us. Not a nice way to end the night.

But I haven't attained my mental goal. The solution is still hiding somewhere, and my determination is fatigued of the journey. Let me slide over into momentary slumber, elbows on the counter, and swabbed puddles flowing to my feet. I'm transcendentaled into a new state. One more dislocated thought, and I could find time forever. If I do, I promise to be mild and retire from fight. Life keeps me thinking about it. My circling mind might just light on something; and then I'd turn into all men: and trade my ferocity for a bland brand of peace. Time takes place here. I'm waiting for the crowd to complete itself. If any man is absent, then my presence is incomplete. I'm only looking for All. When I once have it, you won't notice who *I* am— I'll be less than the stranger whom you met, earlier tonight.

I'll leave you to ponder, and go out alone. I won't stick here for trouble. Here's where I found you, but I don't want to get lost here. We spoke and exchanged our views, for hours among many drinks. We generally were in accord, our companionship made us close from start to now, and here I end it. Go on dwelling. If you find "it," it's my loss for not having remained to share your further research. We end up alone: and loneliness had driven us here. We took up stations together, on these bar stools: and kept a double post, to force our heads past the idea barrier and wind up in the bonus of a strenuous mental award for these pains of illumination we took but quite in vain it seems. They're about to lock up, and the lights are out. The angry bouncer or proprietor is flouncing along toward you, rolling up his sleeves, flinging his apron off, ready to hurl you out of here. *I*'ll slip out, voluntarily. You'll stay for a violent fate. You're trying to shake up the cosmos, and twist time to your own designs? Now you'll be taking your shaking up and a twisting out. That might abort your search, or jolt it to a successful birth. You're trying to put all Time at one: but you've outstayed the safety of lateness, and will be bounced off in penalty. You'll thud on the pavement. A policeman will pick up your scraps. Behind his uniformed shoulder of a bullying blue, the sun will rise into your idea. But will it wake all the dead men, so that you could string them together in one wrapping? You'll die later than they, and before others. We go off sliced up in packs, in small lots. You met *me* tonight, but that's the limiting diet your loneliness can expect. Mankind sweeps on in waves and generations. You're one separated, in your momentary crest—which will dash itself, and join the main. You'll rest in heaven: but mentally, you won't know it. For one whose goal was knowledge, that signs you off a failure. Do you get the picture? That's a snap-identity of you. Then scrap the rest, for it won't fit your unity. Each man carries a stone: and time builds a pyramid. *(Leaves, exits from bar: while proprietor begins to rearrange the remainer, into escorted motion toward the same exit.)*

(While being nudged out of the door, proclaims semi-drunkenly:) That was my partner who left before, hasty with the coward's part. As I'm being hurled out, bodily by force, I do declaim that Culture is here to testify, and a shocked heritage is witnessing this. What's happening *always* took place: now it's being done to *me*. *My* unsolved quest doesn't need a typical bar and disgraceful ouster, but will make its laboratory on the dawning street, where in lumps I'll land. This was all foresaid. I'm the latest to confirm. I'm where all men are: the dead have made me their pet: for I live on, in their stead. *(Is thrown out and door slammed. Voice continues from outside, unseen:)* This ancient indignity is now visited on me. It's *typical*, to be thrown out like this. It was stamped in the right form. By chance, I'm out sprawling. All men *always* felt like this, when exposed to this selfsame sequence. I was prefigured, for all generalities of being in my individual state. No *wonder* I was puzzled: since all conditions are "beyond" me. I so much am, and have so much being, to answer for, that no predicament is personal, My very name-lessness opens me to all names as mine. What I do once, or is done to me, has been a tested action, for a long time. A *future* me will realize this, and use my own transferred memory that can be traced infinitely back. What *I* pass on has come a long way. It's common, from time's beginning to time's end, as the

property of anyone who's a person. Tradition has ruined my individuality. I'm the alienated comparticles of all massed peoples. The cells shift, in replacement: what the cells inhabit—is not replaced. It must prove durable. So *many* pass through. If I'm *one*, I end my count: for when the sum finishes its mounting, it arrives *again* at one. A *different* me: placed not here where I am at this moment of date, but just as well elseplace through any incident of time. I hope *my* version won't let down all whom I represent. But I hope *they*'re doing well by *me*. What a tangle, to play each other!

THE ART GALLERY OPENING WITH NO DRINKS TO LINK THE PAINTINGS AND THE PEOPLE. IT PROVED A COLOSSAL DROUTH

There's nothing so dampening as a dry opening.

Opening to what? My mouth is a dry opening to my stomach, but only when I'm thirsty. A lady has a dry opening when the gentleman doesn't stimulate her. What dry opening do you mean?

An art gallery exhibit. It was the preview, and the guests were by invitation only, except for the majority, who simply heard about it and crashed. You would have thought that a party would celebrate the artist's show. The paintings were being publicly exposed for the first time, so for this special occasion drinks were called for, free alcoholic beverages for those in attendance. But my spirits were dampened, I began to whine, for there were no spirits, or even wine.

How were the paintings?

Too dry. They were all nautical seascapes, but the bodies of water portrayed weren't even wet.

Perhaps that was this artist's little attempt at dry humor.

The whole show was all wet. It was a washout. I didn't soak in the paintings or the people or anything. The people came in like waves, saw there was nothing to drink, and went out like waves, to rejoin the public sea in the street below.

You were high and dry, up there?

As aesthetically also. We didn't drink in those paintings. They didn't flow out to us.

Oh sad opening. Not to get drunk *in life*, is not to get drunk *on art*. The show sank. It drowned. It wasn't even launched.

THE SHRIMP SERVED AT THE PARTY WERE GIGAN-TIC! HERE'S AN EMBARRASSING YARN ABOUT IT

At the swanky party, *the hors d'oeuvres* included enormously large shrimp, brought around by uniformed maids on a tray that also had an enormous bowl of catchup sauce in which guests, via toothpick, may dip their gigantic shrimp. But the shrimp was so large that instead of the toothpicks sticking enough out of them to afford handy grips, they got buried and lost within the vasty depths of such broad-bellied shrimp. So it became necessary for each guest manually—with the fingers unassisted—to dip the groaningly heavy shrimp into the silver catchup sauce bowl. But the heaviness of the shrimp, when re-inforced by the weightiness of the catchup sauce, and coupled with the slimy slipperiness of the glossy sheen of the outside surfaces of the shrimp, caused people's holds to be dragged down; and heavily laden hands would be involuntarily sunk into the bottomless depths of the bowl; and fingertip holds on the shrimp would be loosened; the shrimp would plunge lost to the bottom; and whole hands up to wrists and including soaking sleeves, cuffs, rings, bracelets, and wristwatches, would be thickly laden with the red, syrupy catchup sauce. Oh, the official social embarrassment! Oh unsightly redness! Oh laundry bills to come! Oh wristwatches clogged! Oh mess, unholy!

Yet, the party was an unqualified success. The drinks were generously intoxicating. People gushed in a stagger of confusion. The shrimp episode was forgotten, or brought down to reduced proportions, or portions, that had caught the guests red-handed. A party is a party. That's the right perspective to take. It's a social event. Every guest, and the grand hostess herself, is merely only mortal. That shrinks the shrimp, to shrimplike size.

MORE THAN ONE HELPING

Sol's greed was fantastic. At dinner parties, while other guests were not yet quite through chewing up the tardy remnants of only their first helping of the main entrée course, Sol actually asked for thirds even before he requested seconds: So overleaping was his vaulting ambition, bulging with anticipation before being stuffed in the empirical. One such hostess victim cried out, frankly, "Where's your arithmetic!? To ask for third helping before second helping is to insult the order of sequence and to offend the sacred fundamentals of mathematics, foundation of monetary law and commercial cohesion, the key measure of social reliable trust in a world otherwise given to vague dissensions of opinion, leading to a wilderness of unruly barter and chaotic prefabricated improvising of a makeshift right by sleight of might. Can't you have second helpings, then, in the fit sequence prior to the third?"

"I'm too impatient. I want my thirds *now*—I'm still too hungry to eat my seconds first."

"But you ate your *firsts* first."

"It was hardly enough. That's why I crave the third—to still the final pangs of as yet unabated hunger."

"But what of respect for arithmetic?"

"Arithmetic is by now universal. It'll well survive my momentary mangling of its sacred precedence order. Sequence in pure theory and accepted practice will emerge unscathed, hardly tampered with, in universal procedure. My careless liberties and slipshod desecrating of numerical sequence will barely tarnish the valid worldly code of venerable mathematics, our formidable legacy from steeply established tradition. I'm hungry for thirds in the specific, which strike my fancy and entice my ripe palate.

"For *that* have I a taste; not for dull seconds."

"Then here—help yourself—there—consider that, then, your thirds."

"Oh, it's delicious. Yum yum. Tasting it, I can easily tell how completely preferable this third helping is over what the commonplace second helping *would* have been. Taste will out. I knew what I wanted. I'm justified. Ah, I'm slurping now, I'm wolfing it, even bolting it down, that's how ravished I was. Oh, now there's no more left. I'm still starved. Where's my seconds?"

"Sorry, it's too late for your seconds. If you *insist* on going on, you'll simply, I'm afraid, have to settle for *fourths*, yet."

"What? Fourths before my seconds!? You're crazy! Have you no head for numbers?!"

"I do, as you have a mouth and stomach for helpings and helpings in a heap of the same course. Refill after refill, and still your plate comes down empty—or turns *up* that way. Why, you're a bottomless pit! Are you compensating for a concentration camp fast-past? Or for having been weaned too soon from moma's little nibble? Why, you eat *mounds*! It's a wonder you're not fat."

"On the contrary—I *am* fat."

"Am? Where? You have a slim waist, a narrow, tapering torso, more bone than skin."

"You're blind."

"We obviously differ."

"Where's my second helping?"

"You can't have it before you eat your fourth."

"Oh, you're so orthodox. Your procedure is virtually by rote, to the dull measure of the humdrum. Why be mechanical? Why not skip about, with eccentric abandon?"

"Sol, you're a very trying guest. I have *other* guests to satisfy. You're not the only one, you know. Don't be a selfish pig."

"Give me, then, an *unnumbered* new helping. Let's not fiddle about. I'm ravished. Quick, before I faint."

"The more you've eaten, the hungrier you've become?"

"I'm so famished, I'm desperate. Bother with numbers no more. All I want is to be quantitatively stuffed, in any order. I crave a whole big lot. No more nibbling for me. If these pangs don't go away precariously soon, I'm done for. *Time*, not numbers, is the factor. At once!"

Sol's hostess obliged. He's still at it, eating. He gulps and gulps. When will it all stop? The other guests have gone home, having had their dessert and coffee. Sol is still at the entrée.

Now a new problem! There's no more of that course left, in the bulging casserole-kettle. It's all gone.

So Sol must stop swallowing. He can't gulp at *air*, now. Air is hardly nourishing. He's consumed his food: What's consuming him? For whom or what is *he* the big dish? He can never be had enough of. By whom, or what?

What's eating him? He's gone home. The hostess had no more left, of what he was incessantly eating. But he's in an act of memory. He's not through. He has leftover recollection. It's yummy. How it hits the spot!

What a repast! First by solid, then by afterthought. Matter, and spirit. The corporeal, then the distilled mentalized essence by the glow of thought-fiber.

He's at it, he's still thinking. The saliva beads are pouring. It goes on and on. It's a glowing hot thought. It's food, for the mind.

A PARTY GIVEN BY A SNOB FOR SNOBS. SO EXCLUSIVE, IT'S BARRED TO ALL BUT PEOPLE. THUS PEOPLE ARE ELEVATED, TO THE FIRST RANK.

Anybody who's everybody will be at this party!

Is the party really *that* exclusive?

Yes. It's limited only to people. This has earned the hostess a reputation for being the most exquisite snob. Since nowadays it's unfashionable to be a snob, everybody is avoiding her like the plague.

Then will her party be underpopulated?

Everybody will personally boycott *her*—but not her party.

No, to boycott her party would be carrying personal insult too far. So she'll be cut dead at her own party! The most unpopular one there! She'll be snubbed. But won't her guests be unfair, in their snobbery against snobbism?

By persecuting her, they'll reverse roles with her, and become the snobs they accuse her of being. But meanwhile, everyone can go to the party, provided he's a person. All non-people will be forbidden entry. This discrimination will be strictly enforced. Some gatecrashers will try to "pass" as people, cleverly disguised as lifelong members of the human race. But the hostess is hard to fool. She knows a human being when she sees one. There are all ways of telling. She's always been one herself. So she's *very* sensitive on that score.

Suppose a creature who attempts to crash the party is exposed as a fraud. Will he be evicted?

One can only be evicted if one has already entered. They'll be barred *short* of entry. The hostess will post herself, as sentinel, outside. All imposters as people—people-impersonators—will be pre-ejected from the premises. They'll be publicly embarrassed, with people-approximating humiliation. This will keep the party pure, and freshly pre-purged. People *are* the highest social class, don't you think?

People are the supreme civilizers, the head-mainstays at the helm of the good ship "Society." People, in fact, are the master race.

That's a fascist proclamation.

But people personify *democracy*, as well.

They do. Democracy depends utterly on this particular species.

It does, very generally.

I'll be glad to be among my kind, at the party.

Yes, it's so nice to *belong*. I'm secure, when with my own sort.

So it's a people-honoring party?

Yes. Hence the restricted admission policy, which weeds out all those categorically unfit.

Those misfits! Let them stay out in the cold. How *dare* they presume!

And how nice to be us. Prime people. We *belong*. How pleasant, this impending party. I forgive our hostess. Her snobbishness implies superiority. I join her in that. How together we all are, us people, in our royalty-sharing democracy. We've taken over the earth, in intellectual conquest. Even the insects are scared of us. Birds pause twice, before fouling *our* nests.

True aristocracy confers an elite supremacy on us exclusive snobs. Let's *praise* the hostess, for putting her superiority to the fore. Let's flaunt our kind. A privilege by birth applies to us distinctively. We'll never dilute this true breeding.

Let's all celebrate. We'll drink to it.

Long live our hostess, that benign party-giver. Her blood runs through us all. Though it'll be a mob-scene, it's strictly a family affair. We're all confirmed, by the blessing of a uniform example.

Then we're stamped with a stereotype conformity, by one central pattern that blocks us alike to mere replicas of each other?

Oh, we *do* vary. But what do we vary *from*, is the best stuff. What skin we're all bound to! It's our woven substance. But each one is free, to twist his own latest wrinkle on it. The concentricity is so sure, the eccentricity can pull and yank, if it will; for the thread will hold fast.

To be a person is to be *one*, within *all*?

Supported by the *all*, as a free *one*. Free, yet within. Secure, to be.

OUR HOSTESS, CONFIDENTIALLY REVEALED IN ALL HER CAPTIVATING MIGHT

I

Our hostess was not only our hostess, but a patroness of all the capital arts. Her feature guest was an internationally celebrated musician whose musicality melodized the firmament. He nibbled on crackers all night. (The sound was audible only to himself, because he was a genius.)

But her star guest by far was a poet so obscure that not only were his words ambiguous, but he himself had never even been understood by his own mother. Critics would be forced to psychoanalyze him, to judge his poems on their own merit. To confuse the issue, his sexual habits scandalously inclined toward members of his own race. These inversion tendencies would perhaps prevent his poems from finding a more numerous audience than himself. And what publisher would be intrigued by so exclusive a readership potential? It was likely that the protection of our hostess was all that stood between this poet's stout survival and his impractical wastage as a victim of philistine starvation. Our hostess liked him because he was so ethereally sensitive, which perhaps made up for her coarseness on the grand scale.

The musician and the poet entertained a cordial mutual hatred.

One party is remembered for a great artistic surprise soiled perhaps by a confusing personal outcome.

Our hostess was proud to announce that a major painter was hidden among her guests. "Where is he?", she hunted, scattering groups in her search. As it happened, the painter had faded into his own self-portrait, which was hanging unobtrusively on a wall in front of the alcohol tray which received popular attention. The realistic oil tonalities were brought vividly out by an abstract frame. The painter was given up as lost; the musician and the poet were secretly gladdened not to have their genius threatened by a rival from a disreputable field, since each considered painting to be a bastard art compared to music's legitimacy or the merit of noble and distinguished verse when Her Majesty the Muse was gracious to preside.

II

Our hostess was lavish with food. No guest need go hungry. The poor guests were particularly grateful, but the spoiled rich men in attendance preferred to be entertained by girls in scanty outfits whose dresses subtly revealed a dainty morsel of thigh some six or seven feet above the knee. "Just the right exposure," a professional photographer estimated.

As a further treat for the guests, some genuine circus freaks had been invited. One was the tiniest midget imaginable. He was found choked to death under an artichoke.

A detective was imported, to investigate. Before his findings could formulate the climactic clue, a mushroom he had the imprudence to nibble on poisoned him. The house undertaker (who served our hostess privately on unre-hearse-d occasions) removed the intruding sleuth before a verdict could be obtained. These interludes of suspense spiced her parties, so our hostess ingeniously varied them to keep a guessing-game atmosphere stirring the guests from periodic lapses into the self-installed stench of apathy. "Take nothing for granted here," she commanded, with her manly baritone, below her quaint moustache and the enormous rolls of her heavily-lidded nostrils. (Her heaviness added only more weight to her formidable stature; the better to intimidate the mousier guests and keep them skittishly under her unflagging somewhat flagellant control, with stern military no-nonsense for the disciplined ranks.)

III

The musician and the poet issued each other a challenge, for their enmity had reached the duelling stage. "Choose your instrument!" each gallantly declared, and "Pick your weapon," they corrected under murder-murmurous breath. The musician picked a trombone, and the poet, typically, a typewriter. "That's not fair," our hostess (the referee) intervened, so the combatants had to pick again, to articulate their antagonism with convincing hardware outside of the stylistic rhetoric of art. The vague poet puzzled what might be his last mortal decision. He chose a pen ("It's mightier than the sword,") but his antagonist clutched a grand piano as containing the keys of glorious conquest to turn the scales on a triumphant note to tone down this unequal contest to a harmonic conclusion, restoring the sound sanity of ac-chord. "I'm a-verse to your choice," stipulated the versifier whose pen was dribbling ink in page patterns of poetic innovation which one follower (a junior disciple) instantly imitated to initiate a cult with numerous devotees sprawling onto the improvised bandwagon to precipitate one of the great art movements of our day.

Eventually, the duellists were separated by our hostess, whose decisive "No decision" ended the rash venture with equal laurels on honored brows from the dishonored fray that never simply came off with its vile outlet of bloodshed. "It's outmoded, barbaric, and humanely obsolete," she said apropos the duel as a custom whose civilized use is extinct to modern man in the mercy of progress. Her own salon had almost been the site for one, flurrying the guests with titillation at the dread prospect and slaughtering anachronism.

That novelty had been diverting, with its near-issue of bloodthirsty culmination. Now a lull had momentarily set in, like a vacuum voiding its stifling air with stale exhaust. No stimulant had filled the gap. Sleepiness combatted energy, in some cases, with peaceful results. But as the guests were rapidly being consumed with boredom, our hostess had to think quick of a fresh novelty that would raid ennui with saturation-bombing for bombastic effects. Her wits must sustain the lively reputation of her notoriously envied parties; she would have to dip into a bag of yet uninvented tricks, for the commonplace would surfeit her guests in a haze of drooping satiety, and the party would end well before dawn, which in the hostess circuit is piped as a disaster, and only compulsory suicide could vindicate the consequent ruined career. A morbid contemplation, which determined our hostess on a sensational new ploy.

IV

Who was she, and by where? Her background on the French side presents a historical pedigree of fascinating derivation. She was descended from a tribe called Verdurin, who rose from middle-class trade to aristocratic pretensions. She bribed a Proustian author to carve a niche for her in his book, but was appalled to read that she had been satirically treated as a humorously extreme character; whereupon she disowned all connection with her fictional original, and in a huff gave up reading the works of that literary lion, despite her figuring prominently in his infernal plot of snobbishness which permeated his distinguished volumes linked by first-person guise into structural monumentality and classical modernity. She was glad when that celebrated author died (it was her passive way of getting revenge and living to enjoy it), and now she's a flamboyant party-giver whose taste has often given rise to over-fussy, fastidiously-labored criticism. Her grossness is in fact one of her grand traits, and not easily despised. And she's too formidable for even the most courageous of detractors to take any openly vocal exception; for her parties have the iron-fisted rule of a Rome by imperial Nero, sternly policed with suppressive tyranny. Let no one cross her will, or even have secret dissent, which she'll un-root promptly to castigate with results of excelling harshness (though amusing to onlookers).

No, don't toy with our hostess, she's no one's fool, her stupidity is acutely intelligent, vigilantly cruel, to the calculated malice of a rigid control. What she doesn't know about art is more than atoned for by her cultured approach to people: destroying them without scruple. She finds that it's very practical to be so decisive, for it projects her personality on victims with so strong a spell that they willingly become her guests for a lifetime: giving her parties a popular reputation for adhesive attendance and a strong coterie of regularity, habituated by loyal followers doggedly grateful for such good luck in the privileged sanction of smartly exclusive belonging, membership in the foremost circle of social domination. Our hostess presides, with supreme authority, and takes pains to keep her guests happy. Now they look bored.

V

She rang the bell, calling all to attention. Whisky glasses poised down mid-throat, and food morsels were arrested halfway to the open mouth. Orgies had to disconnect themselves. The bell ranged throughout the household, and brought an orderly heeding centrally in unison by shrill alarm. Our hostess would condescend to make a brief address. Blood rushed to the guests' ears, and without hesitation sobriety replaced drunkenness. Our hostess had a firm hold, chemically and psychically, over the wards of her captivating hospitality. Breath ceased, as she strummed her vocal strings in orchestrated preamble to an announcement that held an audience in hushed thrall, bowing with devout meek submission to what verbal blow was about to befall, alter, and bruise the supplicants in their trembling rows.

The large window blossomed the black electric static of a rush of midnight's jagged lightning that crackled down the pane bedewed with caskets of jewelled tears dropped from the proud monarchy of clouds swooping within range to unburden their chests of broad brutality and aristocratic swagger in a striking gesture to calculate the beholder into frozen terror so pitifully memorable that a chain of shudders will bind the frightened years and impale the heart to the twisting nerves of a stake.

"My dears," began the grand woman, do you have all you need? Don't be too shy to complain. There's been plenty of food and every variety of drink. I trust you've been helping yourselves, without stint. For those unattached men who like a little free lust, I've provided some nice young girls whose costumes are brief enough to insure the stimulation of my myopic or nearsighted guests who might otherwise be forced to rely (as an inferior consolation) on being touched on the tactile nerve (you can guess where), by nearby thighs or fingers, to become excited, which would highly frustrate their *primary* sensual aim, which is to attain the *voyeur's* chaste, detached, but exquisite satisfaction. You see how I pamper to all tastes in my complete catering service which manages to omit not the smallest perversion of which any of my guests is at all abnormally guilty. You come here with diverse appetites, and go away heartily refreshed. You take advantage of my humble self, but to begrudge you would be less than magnanimous. 'So be it,' I say, and must sigh.

"Yes, you gentlemen visitors are cared for beyond my call of duty, you lechers! And for my women guests, I've provided some strong-bodied men and flasks of aphrodisiac perfume to resort to if persuasion is needed to entice the reluctant chosen one. You alluring creatures may then strip in any luxurious bedroom booth and be stroked under conditions of privacy into a panic of panting. My confidential observers and secreted spies have reported some truly turbulent female reactions. If you want ecstasy, my party's the place.

"Even my homosexual guests are royally served with opportunity for their fairy indulgences and lovely-limbed mates to fondly select from an incredibly wide assortment of perverse types. No one's sexual appetite need go wanting, I've seen to every little detail with exasperating patience. I haven't read Freud for nothing. There are even mothers for boys, fathers for girls (though not necessarily from the same family—I'm not *God*, am I?), and incest for everyone so inclined. Goodness, all the morals we violate! I have to bribe a whole police force!

"But the law doesn't interfere, my children, and your pleasures may proceed uninterrupted to all your assorted climaxes for which religion keeps chastising nature and which nature keeps committing in violation of the forbidden, the irregular, the prohibited, the taboo, the illicit, the verboten, obscene, scandalous, dirty, bestial, odious, decadent, naughty, licentious, immoral, unchaste, irreverent, sacrilegious, self-indulgent, lustful, ungodly, infernal, pandering to weakness, diabolical, unsaintly, unrestrained, loose, easy, hot, vice, evil, bad, and wrong. All these are allowed to you, under my supervision, which has been extraordinarily lenient and permissive. (When have you seen me employ my punitive prerogative?) I could be a usurer in gratitude debts, did I so choose! Under who else's roof is your freedom so joyously familiar, generously indulged, promiscuously gratified, boundlessly pleased whatever notion your whim may take in undirected form owing its amorphous origin to the diffused zone conspicuously located where the groin flashes erotic signals to send off waves of passion, love, desire, and sentiment in search, for the appropriate partner of gentle congenial congenital genial gentility for the glowing genitals offered in return? 'A mate for everyone' is my

motto. I could win the Presidential nomination on that plat-
form, and sweep into office as easily as Venus into the heart of
Mars in pre-Cupid nativity. 'A mate for everyone!': That's our
party slogan. And easily exchangeable for fickle variety's appetite, you jades of jaded indecisive collective lust without human differentiation! You mob of beasts in the general, with no
individual fidelity or angelic constancy! You blind instruments
of fornication's unerring instinct! Ah, you herd of pilgrims to
pioneer the body's ever-virginal wilderness! You trail-blazers
in the wild rut of sameness! The invariable routine in dull sex's
alleyway.

"Pause for drinks. Refresh yourselves. Now I continue.

"My hospitality by no means includes celibacy! Of *monks*
and *nuns* there are *none*; *monk*eys, rather. That's who you are!

"Or that's *what* you are!: you lowlife!

"Yes, I *know* you have *hearts*, you dear things! And not under
the belt, but in your bosoms. You darlings, how welcome you
are here! My house is the enchanted stage for romantic drama
acted out for real, in person, by you! By direct tools and straight
methods, too! The libido and the id are outrageously naked,
here, and are out for all they can get, obeying nature's prompting with throbbing alacrity! Oh the spasms (collected under my
roof with incessant regularity) would supply an unwound clock
with enough heartbeats to run a bloody year of triple overtime
and still tick the tock in continuous and minute observance
of seconds! And the glandular secretions grossly netted on my
teeming beds, if poured over the Sahara Desert, would make it
an ocean equipped with sperm whales and eggs hatching into
fertilized monsters in a slime of flooding generations! Thank
Providence I've provided contraceptives to abort progeny as
ugly as yourselves and malformed! Birth has *already* bungled,
getting *you* here! Repugnant squirming things! Detested as you
are, I place you under my loving control, the better to abhor

you with protective ardor! You common scum of my precious patronage!

"Yes, I know you like it here, otherwise you wouldn't come so often. (You're free, I don't prevent you either from not arriving or from going once you've come.) Yes, you're addicted to me! I spoil you with an undeserved way of life that sultans would envy and millionaires vainly emulate though unlimited be their resources! Oh what fortune is yours, if you only knew!

"Under whose auspices? Mine! What thanks are owing to me! I reject them, my friends; we're all intimate, and I *share* your equality for *myself*, as well. We're all one family here, as I must maternally remind you. I'm your matronly sister, humbly among your ranks! I have Open-Gutter, for you to crawl in! I throw my doors open, for pity of your breed! In you invade, and hang your stink up all over the place! You're given the run of the joint, and make yourselves at home in liberal repugnant audacity, insolence, insubordination, horrific arrogance, like a perfect pestilence! Better you had remain unnamed, you anonymous mongers of shame!

"You're deep into my favor, you know, and the bounty is infinite! You bask in the bulging coffers of my hospitality. Food, drink, and sex you glut yourselves on, you swilling swine! Oh this contemptible breed of mine! Irrepressible savages doting on my civilized means with their draining inexhaustibility: like vile pups of mongrelly origin nursing on the teats of a sacred cow, meanly sucking the gilded nectar of my polished vitals!— my exquisite fluid gulped by infinitesimal whelps! For *what* do I donate my fountain of glorious milk? The least things of life in their revolting animation, the barely oozed spawn of paternal vegetables! Their disgraceful lineage, and they the loathsome offspring of. And to me—*Me!*—they come!

Creatures of dismal darkness. I dearly adore you all, and do what I can within my generous means. I provide you with chambers for love, and the sustenance of delirious sense for your soulless bodies. I'm only a rather privileged servant serving the lowliest masters. You won't condescend to tip me, I hereby warn you! If you dare to thank me, lashes will scourge you; my hospitality contemptuously refuses your concerted or individual gratitude, whether mass or singular. Be my carnal guests, and know where you are. This is a den of love: make it and like it. Organize the orgies, and begin at once! Nobody excused on the grounds of fatigue! Do it again, if you did it before! You may not omit: you must commit! This is my order! Off with your clothes, and embody my decree! Personally! No one to abstain! No cheating! Young and old, all at once, in whatever group or partnership. On with it! No shirking! Obey, don't pray! *You* are my entertainers! Acquit yourselves well, servile stunters! Leap to it, ogres! Devour, be devoured, and be the consumed consumers, and the glandular flames organ the infernal fueling to pile the stake of ashes up, oh my martyrs in a heap! Ah, action makes a life useful, and repeated age is twice as youthful. Rage, you communal pyre! slake those hot bodies of their groins' gushing thirst! Entwined and writhing, those saints of festival heat, the solemn plungers interlocked in playful patterns of sprawling indignity. Ah, call in the resident priest and let him perform Mass, which holy office shall fasten such dull beasts in a throes of benediction and a veneer of grace. And blessing's garb, exterior to their inner stink!"

VI

How tired we were, with enforced indecency! So difficult to rise, that mattresses were left under us and group sleeping was our next joint activity. We had surrendered our will, and were not responsible. What our hostess had given, she would take away, as her own time disposed her, and the fruitful ripeness of her wisdom. We must carry out what she ordained, and seek not to reason, but strive piously to obey. That was sweet, and absolved us of so much. We were granted the status of children, and in meek innocence were holy in the protected righteousness of the sanctity she upheld, authorised, and would defend as her duty charged her in the obligation of high office. We were that to which she administered, and her calling was one we must honor without protest; her jurisdiction was liberally for our benefit, though conservatively it would keep us ruled without power of self-determining representation. We were her charges, she was our government, insurrection was not possible, her single bidding must be our submissive consensus. Despite the many consolations, our pride would privately remind us what tiny scope it was given, and how hilariously hopeless would be our pretense to dignity or minimum assumption to human self-respect on the crystal scales of a neutral conscience.

VII

Not always were those parties base. A collection of highly refined guests reversed the coarse grain, supplanted the boorish with intellectual glitter and a staple of artistic distinction that did credit to our hostess as an organising agent of keen selectivity. She had no rival among other so-called hostesses, her galaxy was of the first magnitude as a sun-eclipser. Her foremost favorite of all musicians favored her with the staunch loyalty of being a regular guest! How he could make music sing! His performances with whatever instrument (versatility was his forte) drove tears in sentimental streams to her auditorily acute eyes. Her ears would have to be blocked with cotton if the intensity threatened to damage her nerves and impair her rock-hard sanity. Her private physician was in constant attendance with his remedial kit and suave advice that a charlatan would have been incapable of even conceiving. She was a culture addict, and every guest was obliged to develop an unfailing creative gift.

Omnipresence would be practical, but as yet she wasn't skilled enough at it. Therefore she couldn't check to insure that her edict was being successfully imposed on all guests, whose latent talents must be reared, nurtured, and harvested to delectable fruition. Everyone had to be creative on faith; there was no test, only this ominously benevolent trust naively assumed with vast impartiality by our relentless hostess, whose thunderous intent was withheld by her streak of mercy which she would wield with incalculable poise and immovable control.

We were spared, and took endless trouble to offset any prompting of her prodigious wrath, averting it with every trick of courtly diplomacy and gallant fastidiousness known to the sly stratagem of survival. She was wise to all our moves, but played dumb on occasion. We mice could get away with certain antics, when the yawning cat closed tight her eyes of slanting treachery-deception-detection as a magnanimous gesture of forebearance, forgiveness, and other Christ-inspired virtues scripturally endorsed with biblical text. Our hostess was greatly meek, for withholding the might of magnificent vengeance on us petty offenders. In default of our *major* sins. We were toys, to her puppeteering scale; and had to string along, under her divine guidance. We had abdicated choice, and strutted on a stage of weakness the pompous posturings and shadowy puffings and trumped-up expostulatings pumping our poses to mime deeds of great valor in mind or might, fed by dictation of our hostess, whose sponsorship of our fiction embroidered instant mythology on fabrics of our puny intent, hoisting fabulous engravings on scrawny underpinnings, giving bold relief in stirring legend to the scrawn and strut of our feeble basics carved of great main to momentous burlesque. It was all one cheat, but our hostess dignified it.

VIII

We paltry underlings and futile things were revived, one party, from despicable absorptions by our rallying hostess, whose lofty preoccupations would redeem us to noble conversions. What latest fad would she improvise to enlighten our edified illumination from our dark sensual corners? Her mastery broke out into cunning voice and consummate speech:

"This is my house, and I won't tolerate stupidity in it! I see to it that you're sexually relieved, in order not to be distracted from the more imaginative concerns, those chaste pursuits of the spirit of man, whether verbally clad or visually garbed, or musically robed. I have celebrities who represent each field with expertise and noted authority. They're under my wing, and you be under theirs. Consult them, to excel in some worthy craft. Food and sex and drink only amuse our *skin*; remember that we have souls to tend, spirits of mystery that must be instrumentally cultivated. Apprentice yourselves freely into the hands of my artistic experts. They're not here to be idly gawked at. Their booths are scattered throughout my broad expanse of rooms at handy intervals for your frequenting convenience. Your custom is solicited; under duress of penalty for loafers who abstain in the complacency of philistine shrinkage. We're all here to be artistically active, and I'll breach no exceptions to this gravely reformist law. I'll do good to you, even if I have to kill you at it.

"My uniform order applies to all, whatever your original endowments may have been. I warn you, go seek out my crew of celebrated masters of their respective crafts, you can locate them with ease or miss them with foreknowledge of a hell of peril, so I simply say 'Find them or else.' A word to the wise will usually suffice, unless you'd like to witness my blazing severity in chastisement of offenders. No, you wouldn't, would you?

"Here's opportunity to learn a promising skill—*several* are obligatory, in fact. I advertise an enterprising set of influential masters whose experience will keep you in untold benefits. Your debt would take even your grandchildren's lifetimes to repay at a pauperising rate of grateful interest for your delightful introduction to art's mystic cult. These exponents of culture's intriguing arts are waiting to initiate you at an undelayed instant. This unlimited offer of incalculable reward is open immediately, those solemn priests you'll find cheerfully available. My household is lit with them at deeply committed intervals on altered shrines devotional. Their canopied stalls can be recognised by signs appropriately designating the wares of each as an educational service to train your higher faculties until you, too, may attain genius rank. Why not? It only requires a slight stretching of capacities, minor adjustments by the skull's nervous network in sympathetic collusion with the heart. Then your status will be lifted, to the creative pinnacle!

"Not by surgery, alchemy, witchcraft, or any phony fakery, but by strenuously difficult means: You must be genuine advocates at painting, composing, writing, and other *real* work! This is no den of pretense! Let no dilettante dare disgrace my strict abode where crafts are *plied*, not *im*plied. No forgers need apply, nor Sunday painters nor poetasters nor frittering dabblers frivolously given to insignificant dissipation that symbolically approximates the immortal accuracy of true productivity! No hacks, no scribblers, no mediocrities. No commercial prostitutes in advertising 'compromise' nor potboiling popularizers, nor academic critics, nor society collectors nor bohemian pretenders nor professional eccentric nor off-beat spongers nor group-activity exploiters nor hysterical culture-maniacs nor organizational diffusionists, institutionalizers, business brokers, entrepreneurs, speculators, promotion diplomats, television personalities, controversy opportunists, obstructive appreciators, psychoanalytic apologists, sociological interpreters, Marx-manipulators, Freud-fraudulents, easy-life careerists, or flimsy hangers-on in art's legitimate rat race, nor soulful spiritualists nor technical craftnicians, nor occult ivory-towering cultics nor administrative patronizing bland open-liberal-mindedness, nor progressive recognition, and we don't want lazy theorizers nor other evasive parody-mockers of art's high purpose. You must all toe the line, and shit the nonsense out of you. It's ever easy to fake on the sidelines, the world is spacious there for wide variations on pretense and gimmicks of invented show for impressive aping of an ego's duplicate pose. None of that is the real thing!

"I'm a particular hostess! I only collect the genuine article, and dispense with rot on the rubbish heap. I'm tired of worldly banality. I want an *exclusive* gathering—distinction on *merit*, not claim! To be frank, I'm *very* exacting. I'll only have *real* artists, *practicing*! Anything less is rejected in the inferior pile for lesser hostesses to pick from. I won't be troubled with any but *great* followers: I've no time to waste. Now, attend me!

"You're all inducted into my vast creative array. I greatly bother, but for greater results. Heed me, for this terrific news that will metamorphose you from an evolutionary beginner to undergone mastery in leaping stages to undying fame with only the rudiment of a transition!

"We're all gathered in the main immense room of my world-size house. We're not cramped. There's room for everyone to explore his major assets (untapped as yet) in the more imaginative of man's inventive endeavors, which sacrifice practical use for beautiful truth and emphasize the civilized prizes of the soul's explorative venture into life's richer meanings of regarded essences as interpreted by modes, mediums, and vehicles of understood code. Why should I elaborate? I'll come at once to my point.

"Spiritual values above material ones, of *course*. How, though, arrived at? Through *tools*, my children!

"I command you to be artists, and I mean to back it up, for words, paint, and sound to come crashing through! If you for a moment believe my words are idle, suspend your doubt and listen into conviction while I tell what in deed I've furnished your budding geniuses with, in the way of very useful implements! (This is no high boast, but instrumental for getting works done.)

"There are many of you, but why should that have hindered me? The challenge was thus more generously solved; and my munificence was vastly translated into a booming abundance.

"What does art? Answer: Head and tools. You already *have* heads, so what have I donated?

"Look about, and from the room's enormity single out your focus of approval on what I must dramatically point to, as the trained spotlights shift to lift your grateful eyes of surprise:

"Behold! It's here! On the huge central table, I've supplied all the tools you need, however intricate your creative speciality or experimentally devious:

"Pens, pencils, typewriters, paint brushes, canvases, easels, musical instruments, reference libraries, privacy, inspiration, security, peace, incentive, skill, ideas, inventiveness, judgment, taste, models, precedence, tradition, tubes of paint, pastels, crayons, turpentine, wiping rags, huge color reproductions, smocks, draftboards, measuring utensils, plenty of light, the appropriate atmosphere, cameras, photographic equipment, vast studios stuffed full of total spatial freedom for you, rolls of film, enlargers, darkrooms, plates, screens, projectors, overhead lighting, skylight, musical scores, pendulum beat-setter, rhythm regulators, tune finders, tone sounders, key-quickeners, volume mufflers, sheets of notation, busts of eminent composers, long hair, temperamental outbursts, long trances, duplicators, reproduction machines, carbon, stencil, rhyming dictionaries, clay, chisels, marble, wood, armature wire, drapery, a feeling for solid volume, blueprints, contracts, diplomas, engineering counsel, rich clients, a free hand, blank checks, blueprint sheets, rich vellum, advising specialists, co-operation from town planners, municipal sponsorship, liquidation of rivals, unbeatable readymade reputations, fame and eminence: and whatever else you need. This is a studio workshop. Roll up your sleeves, doff jackets, don frocks, off with high heels, get consultation, and work prolifically. Start turning out the masterpieces. You'll be judged on performance, on what you produce. You can't get away with hot air or a boastful promise. My monitors will check your projects, my foremen will rate your process, my supervisors will mark all progress. Hectic activity; and even *my* voice, on its soothing soar of encouragement and rallying note of stress, will cease, to furnish you with peace. Composers get private sound-proof booths, and no one may be disturbed. Typewriters installed that rattle silently, and even the sculptural utensils are muffled. A mute greatness has pierced our air. Fulfill it."

IX

Trembling, we all worked. The glare of our mistress prevented shirking; for her omnipresence had become an imperative factor, and was now so surpassingly developed that rather than face paranoia at her reprimands however imaginary, we ferociously applied ourselves to persevere with unremitting diligence, knocking off what we hoped would be sufficiently good work to vindicate our apprentice indebtedness to her sublime support of artistic endeavor. To risk disappointing our patroness and have having her disapproval crash down on us in harsh peals of censure, would daunt the last coward of us; *to fail* being far out of the question, we *had* to succeed, and we did: establishing our city as the leading center in art and literature the world over, and our hostess' circle as beyond dispute the one totally untarnished with imperfection of any salon since standards were ever absolute.

It was a fertile period of work and uncontrollable happiness. Aesthetic history now had to alter itself retrospectively, for *we* had come along and reversed the declining spiral; we *were* the Classical age: and preceding eras were decadence. *Ours* was the Renaissance, and not any previous.

X

I was the resident novelist. I was provided with a theme index and a character-etymology list, as well as a plot manipulator to mechanically regulate my narrative with infallible guidance. Party after party, our artistic standards slipped, and even our hostess's regenerative hysteria wasn't rapid enough to repel our steady decline from our excellent peak of a few parties before. Our lapse was unaccountable, and she wore the tragic look of the dictator whose provinces are overrun with revolution and repudiation of authority, getting out of hand and despoiling her throne of its methodically assembled empire. Her systematic construction of a genius factory was being undermined by decay from within, as she stood by, her smoking whip unable to stem mediocrity's onrushing tide that mortally washed over our brief sojourn with immortality.

The few true products of our collective summit, accomplished by that rare "once" of inspiration, were the property of our hostess; as she reconfiscated what she had put in. My one outstanding novel was submitted to her rights, and indeed entitled to her name. Now we were only party guests, for the limelight of momentary greatness had been dispelled and we were clicked back to our former realms with the enchantment washed creatively out from our large ascensions. Our level retrieved us, and our dull retreat was official.

Oh so our roles were hackneyed. Consoled by memories of high departure, a paradise we were expelled from, and the drop emphatic of our towering. A romance that flirted with a permanent lovely ideal; but deceived, debunked past reclaim or recognition; and now Regret for not keeping up what once really was, is our sunken limbo where our recession consolidates. Darkly to take stock, in the cold perspective of sober recapitulation. A winter having been wrenched from summer's fleeting corpse.

XI

Nostalgia our one glory. Stupidity our current prize.

Who caused the bungling? Our hostess alone was responsible. Now prepare her slow persecution.

Her glib bulk minces these hulking, parroting words (now impatiently received by her smouldering guests):

"For those whose enthusiasm is books, I have my poet-in-residence, who is well-read in addition to being creative, and who is well versed on most things worth reading for the articulate purposes of conversation in the general run of literary information, and he knows personally some other famous writers, whose private lives he'd be pleased to gossip about if you grant him the request with a scandalized look of intense absorption in his deflation of these stuffed characters. (They don't attend my salon, so what good can they possibly be, reputations to the contrary?)"

Were we really forced to listen? We all hated her.

No one as yet dared to revolt. Her spies were scattered among us. We couldn't tell them from ourselves.

But we were seething. She could detect that, it was quite transapparent. How could she put down our growling resentment, or quell our hidden insulted rage? The blame must unfairly fall to her.

She had granted us something magical that had then been retracted: not by her, but despite her. Our power had been ripped away, suddenly withdrawn, after suddenly bestowed. She had refused, in advance, our gratitude for the gift we gained; but could she redact our surly undercurrent of wrath, now that the gift, being lost, must be replaced by the most obvious scapegoat that logic could glare at to appoint fury's fuse to, in a palpable rebound flaring the malice of our joint vengeance on our benefactress? Spiteful vehemence, not detached renunciation, would spur our rebellion. Never would that hour of art be regained; its loss smarted, and would damn our hostess.

XII

She had conferred a special power on our poor ability; but had not made permanent that exalted property. It had drained away, and her pain must pay the day. Her neglect in providing that our abrupt magic would preservatively be maintained, now loosened her own magic spell over us, and our captive bonds would soon allow escape through that burst pipe or leakage. Her hold was broken, the feudally imposed contract of rapport snapped; though we were her loyal guests, and she still presided as our party hostess with ostentatious splendor and her brash flamboyance that now had the dazzling spectre of artificial tinsel and the false note. The charm had subtly worn off, and was no more.

We kept a regular attendance, to allay suspicion; we had dwindled into her normal vassals on the surface; but the eruption was monstrous beneath, and sought no less than her entire destruction as our only satisfaction that retaliation would supply in mutinous glee. The contemplation of this rewarded our subsided living with almost intolerable pleasure. For our hostess to be doomed—and by *us!*—was so keen an intellectual irony that we re-imagined it in various forms, turning it over like a revolving chicken on a spit, a rotating morsel of scrumptious grill for our gluttonous examination at all savory points sauced by the high spice of sadism with perverse cunning of appetite. The odor thrilled our nostrils, the dish was set before us to wake a fasting corpse to his gourmet incarnation in delirious relish for his risen feast back into life. The delicious repast to rip past the resounding resurrection and famish death forever by stuffing life full. The cannibal stew of our hostess in the bulging haughtiness of her pot was a hungry prospect for as many cooks to prepare as guests there were, and if elaborately spoiled, would make a crusading meal in guts convulsed by her machinations. Devout we've been, and devouring mean to be.

Our saliva is whet, and teeth prancing to the kill.

Meanwhile, her bounty holding out, we clean up her table with edible goods, consume her strong beverages, and conduct our orgiastic rites with primitive savagery, under her all-permissive roof, between walls of expensive reverberation.

By our bored hordes, her hoard and board are ravaged, till by her replenished from the locked stocks and groaning larder. And her money meets an equal match in us, her ravenous crew with greed, gluttony, bestiality, and drunken license to drain her goodly substance like swine on a spree. How we swill, how we abuse. And let elegant refinement abode itself at a more genteel hostess's house of crowded luxury popular by invitation to parasites.

That ugly dame! No remorse for us nor sissy shame; only exploitation, in our plundering rampage, spreading its muck of vengeance on the glittering rugs amok on a mocked choreography of traced stampede in riotous design wasting the stores of generous plenty by mobs defiant with gross ingratitude to squander all our hostess has or can own or supply, rowdy against her service and prodigal with what she lavishes. And toss moderation to the pets, for our fare is no mean extreme, and takes all of our efforts just partially to exhaust. And with each *other* we make free, in forms that various fornication takes on its murder-course on the biting bolt of intensity. No expense is spared; our bounteous hostess amply provides, while we take. Her giving is carelessly met, and as easily spent. And "More, still more!" our complaining chorus wildly claims, not bothering with *demand*'s tact or the politeness of *request*. Our grovelling is past, and our wants audible.

Her thundering walls and crashing chandeliers chaotically maul our hostess, as the windows give way and the hard ceilings fall. Her reign topples, for her sprawling empire riots. The queen's crown keeps reluctant company with her head it sits precariously on, and that manicured hair runs unruly disorder at her wild, heating temples.

"I'll test who was loyal to me," she determines, calling for her pampered musician and her fussed-over poet. The artist is hidden in his painting, slung on the wall. And who else will boost her? Now that emergency has clanked the alarm, she'll find out the ones who'll return her support, and give back a little after having so much received. Our hostess was in need, and where were her staunch defenders, rising to her gritty peril with grateful allegiance and with brave devotion? The holy protection is reversed, and our hostess stands distressed; her power is crumbling, and whose patronage will turn a timely service into her crucial rescue?

THE HANGOVER AND HALO OF A POST-MORBID SESSION TO VINDICTIVELY FUMIGATE THE PREVIOUS NIGHT'S PARTY AND PRE-PURGE THE FOLLOWING NIGHT'S EQUALLY OBNOXIOUS PARTY HELD MORALLY OBLIGATORY TO ENDURE IN RIGHTEOUS OPPORTUNISM: THEN *THAT* PARTY, AND STILL ANOTHER ONE, ATTENDED BY DELIRIUM AND A RESHUFFLING OF THE EGO'S DISORDERLY CONSPICUOUS MORAL SOCIAL ROLE OF GUILT BY ACCUSATORY COMPARISON WITH ONE'S FELLOW BEINGS

(Scene: Indoors, the evening after.)

Have you recovered from last night's party?
Just about, but my all-day hangover is still hanging over.
Over who?
(Looks above his own head:) Over me.
Well, I hope it controls its bowels.

(Silence)

There were lots of people at the party.
Did you talk to *new* ones, or those you *already* knew?
Being both progressive and conservative, I did both.
    Then you're a political coward, when it comes to parties, as you straddle the hedge and hedge on which saddle.

(Silence)

Did the party provide scandal and gossip?
No, but plenty of beer and wine.
    Don't be facetious. People interest me, and parties expose them, betray their darker secrets in the muddy alcoholic glare. Let's review the party, by holding a post-morbid.
    Yes, we'll have a cosy post-morbid session.
    Good. *(Looking at the imaginary point just above his own head:)* You can come down now, Mister Hangover.

(Silence. Hours later:)

Have we finished conducting our post-morbid?

Yes, and the party guests we discussed have come off disgustingly.

In *themselves*, they're not bad: but they just won't bear talking about.

Not by *us*; their characters crumble to ruin under our distant haze of scrutiny, the conjectural malice of our most unkind analysis.

It serves them right, for having exposed themselves as scurvy victims to our scurrilous survey.

But by comparison, *we* came out well.

Yes, retrospect has been kind to us.

Our personalities have been neither impaired nor slandered by it.

Our post-morbid has, in fact, substituted a nimbus halo in the stead or place of where was poised my hovering hangover some time before.

Then our post-morbid has elected you an angel!

Yes. This vindictive contrast, that crowns me so, is the only reason the host invited those other guests whose characters we were forced to mercilessly assassinate. They're a devil's lot, to assure my ascendancy of angelic saintly martyrdom to last night's disreputable party. How well my virtue is defined, once our mingling has identified those scum!

You soar exalted. Is there another party tomorrow?

Yes, we're invited. For research and compassion, not for the vainglory of righteousness.

What drink will be offered, or manifestly available on the democratic table?

No mere wine or beer, but whisky itself!

Ah, and unescorted girls to meet and later seduce?

With exasperating abundance, a splendiferous assortment of choice!

Then let's go. *(Looks above other's head to notice a conspicuous absence:)* What happened to your halo?

I've had it sent to the cleaners. Our latest dialogue exchange has sullied it somewhat.

Will it be ready for tomorrow's party?

I'll leave it off: better to disguise myself, with unassuming apparel.

Why?

Oh, for opportunity to maneuver unsuspected by my test victims. If they knew of my recently innate superiority, their unnatural adjustment would upset the typical norms of their behavior, and distort my experimental standards. I must keep some background constants, to detect the random variables, thus unimpairing the severity of my judgment. Science is an exact study, and will admit of no subjectivity. The researcher should stand neutral: so my halo will be left home. Sociology will be rife for the vital truth, tomorrow night.

Will we acquire a new hangover, to necessitate a stiffer post-morbid?

Only should our moral superiority be brought to question, our eminent rectitude be held to doubt, our unassailable position be daringly defied or threatened, our supreme integrity be discredited, our dignity be implicated, our stature desecrated, our natural advantages resentfully suspected and our esteemed reputation flagrantly violated. Then our post-morbid would give us conversational revenge on our absent maligners, whose offenses must be verbally vindicated and categorically indicted in the secure sanctum of our recapitulation.

But first to the party, to gather the odious material that we'll purge privately later.

Yes, to the party: evil's hideous cesspool, revoltingly on exhibit.

But should we inflict self-suffering on us?

Let's enjoy it, while it's there.

(Silence. Two nights later:)

(Indignantly, exasperatedly:) I knew it! My halo's back from the cleaners, but it's shrunk to a useless degree—as though it had been made of inferior cloth.

Then you'll have to *assume* your moral privilege, and the benediction it confers on your esteemed, inviolable self.

All right. But what's invisible is unconvincing as a symbol for what it transparently must uphold.

But isn't the *fact* of your virtue pure enough, not to borrow its emblematic stage-prop?

Virtue must be *seen*, and *then* believed: even by the halo's would-be wearer.

Lacking that, are you evil then?

Beyond respite, and too far out for redemption's rescuing hand.

But what was your sin, at our party last night?

That everybody behaved as impeccably as we did. Their characters are invulnerable to our methodically prepared assault. We're no longer holy, for we lack our contrasting foil.

But spiritually, we're undefiled as ever, though without the concretely embodied halo.

That's no matter. Virtue is by virtue of a hierarchy of graded ranks and degrees on a systematic scale of merit. An equal virtue in democratic alignment eradicates the superiority principle, on which my prestige has been solemnly founded to upholster the intricate mechanics of my self-respect.

Then Christians shouldn't go to parties.

No. And why did God invent guilt, if He gave us pleasure?

And why conspicuous self-comparison with others at parties?

Whisky and hangovers, haloes and women—and the post-morbid as a remedial device for bolstering the precarious balance of ego: the sorry scheme of things below. Let God uproot His plan, and found a new social system more in tune—

—Oh stop it, you halo-less beast!

But—

—And stop dragging God's name in lieu of a deficiency of party scandal. You're tampering with Heaven!

But *Heaven's* interference is omnipresent, in our sordid lives.

Would you better rather be dead?

No, such a rash solution—

—Then stop abusing the Almighty! Censor your narrow arrogance! Your pride is artificially cultivated. Your concern with a social role—

—Then not a single more party!

All right! Be a recluse! Be a hermit in isolation, and Nature will impose a gregarious punishment on you.

You've got me convinced! When's the next party?

Tonight, in half an hour, if you're casual about preparation.

To hell with preliminaries! I'm roaring to go!

(Silence. Following night:)

What's hanging over you?

Everything conceivable, with one exception: a halo.

Did you enjoy the party?

A wonderful bunch of people!

And no complaint?

Contempt for my fellow men is a sacrilege against the sanctity of self. That party was a paradisiacal piece of hell!

Good. Are you restored to cosmic unity?

To an indistinguishable extent!: I no longer differentiate.

Then your consciousness isn't laden with too much self?

No. I'm all people.

But not scandalously so?

Oh, guilt is communally owned. It's no one's private property.

Good. You're absolved, then.

WHAT'S A PARTY WITHOUT PEOPLE? ANSWER: WHEN IT'S OVER.

Oh, the party was just wonderful tonight. The people were flowing in between the drinking. Among the people, many of them seemed to be women, and in fact even were. How's that!, for the identities some people have.

The drinking often caused confusion, and in some cases even *was* confusion. The confusion was driving people among and between the other people—or was *driven*. The confusion often got out of hand. As for the people, they and their confusion often got confused even more. The words went out, the drinks went in, at the same mouths in most cases, including the remaining cases as well. But some people were even sitting. Thus, the walking-standing ones were only at the comparative height advantage and mobility-opportunity, by comparison with their seated cousins of our all-the-same human species. By now, the party was in more than high gear. The hosts and hostesses kept out of the way, while the guests surged and by sheer numerical quantity got mixed up and swept up by the same people in shifting renewals of here now and there later, this head bobbing there, now surging here, all in the dense pack. What could you say?, after all that. More important, what did you say *during* all that? For the swarms were swarming, and all the egos were arming. Anger dotted the room in little groups, but in other rooms the feelings got relieved and fell swiftly ahead from the almost stifling congestion of people packed head to head in seas of different heights, while at the corners with backs to walls the soft seating was, with its level of underground conversation or undersea, as the words were lifting and the drink was falling forward and the people in mixed batches stayed mixed and eventually re-met, stray couples would become united after partitioning by division, while drinks were lost count of, or in the confusion were well forgotten but would emerge at mouth level where all the conversation was. Some women were more attractive than others, but some were even married or with very close boyfriends that seemed to guard them from a distance. All in all, this party hummed at paces, while the people filled it out. They had to. The drinks were all the way at one end, two hired bartenders with a bottle-filled table on white cloth, while maids with *hors d'oeuvres* trays kept getting lost, but were recovered the next time around and little food plucked by eager fingers for the appropriate mouths corresponding through the same bodies of the plucking fingers. Some food got offered, however: this hand to that mouth. But the biggest trading and dealing was in words. The words were always there, at all times.

Some of the words even clouded issues. Or was that just cigarette smoke? In the blur, there was a maze. Through the maze, there was still another blur. But people did get places, but all within the same party. By now, however, a few dribbling guests were being decimated from the broader ranks of those who still were remaining; so though the rooms filled out, a dwindling number only remained, from once so swollen at the peak and surge of the crowd at stifle. A crowd is only constituted out of individuals. An individual is only one person. But enough of such kind, and you may have a whole party, to celebrate something by your organization, a business firm, maybe it published a book, so the press got invited, plus publicity gala. Magazines and newspapers and even radios had their representatives there, and the industry of publishing. The money outlay was considerable. The party was being invested in. Word would get round. This would lead to a network of eventual profit. Wasn't profit the prime business motive? At the monetary basis, of it all.

By now, the party was almost no more. You could see more and more empty floor space, wall space, seat space; spaces were opening up everywhere, fewer people the less spaces, if you lingered you could see this subtle transition. The room of the bottle-filled table was now closed, the door thereof: you couldn't get in. So you shuffled around, glad to see your glass was still more than half full: enough to last you, for the duration. You can't count—you lost track—of what number of drinks this is your last of. It *is* your last. The corporate host and hostesses have ensured that, by having the door to the barroom closed shut. It was a pointed hint, and you'd better take it. It's even getting darker, some lights went out. You'd better go and get your coat. Where have the pretty women gone? Some have even lingered. The ones who are not pretty are mostly older—maybe they used to be pretty. If so, that's all past, by now.

Party, party, where have you fled? You're gone from what you were. I was there with you, in those rooms up in the building. I'm obviously now alone in a *different* building, miles off in the same city. The city unites us, but time has paved a wedge, while location has moved off and only memory brings you back, partial and mental, while the scene isn't the same. The scene is lost. There is now no party. Here I am, while there's no party. I can tell. There *was* one. It was, it was. But where is the was that was? The party with the women, and all the confused drinking on the pouring forth of legs flowed? Flown. There's no more confusion. It's all too clear, now. We are in attendance at the party's absence. All of us, the whole body of us, I'm a yanked off part, where is that "we"? I'm still. There's a party going on. The wonder of it is there. It fills my head. The rooms *were* filled. Only my head remains. The party was wonderful, thank you. A delightful social occasion. Also angry, also commercial. And the roving eye. The fumed mouths. The waxing words. The words even now, lost of sound, but some meaning trails. Communication. That's what the party achieved. What are we, without it?

I'm without it now. Ghosts have settled. Bring back the party. Or await a new one. Not the same, but new.

(The two-paragraphed title that comes following in conclusion the pre-ceding bulk and body of work:)

THE PARTY IS OVER. BUT IT REALLY WAS. THAT'S HOW IT WAS ABLE TO BE OVER NOW.
OVER HERE, IN MY HEAD. NOT OVER THERE, WHERE IT WAS. OVER WHAT, DID IT PASS? OVER ITS OWN SELF. AND INTO THIS.

THE REGRETFUL APOTHEOSIS; THE FALLING BACK INTO MAN'S DELIGHT

Finding myself unloved was tempting to self-pity. I gave in to that temptation. Meanwhile, I sought to undo the self-pity via direct means: finding a loving loved one. I had each of my friends find a prospect for me whom I would meet as a mutual dinner guest. This took up most evenings each week for weeks. Besides that method, I found about any weekend parties going and religiously went to each one, where I'd scour the place for un- or loosely-escorted prospects available as loving and loved ones. Perhaps my being so obviously "on the hunt" scared off these so desired potentials. Or in some cases my searching may have smacked of an unattractive desperation to ward off those who, rather than being "pressed", would prefer to choose a more contented man, a less easily satisfied one, someone so esteemed as not to have that "starved" look. So my campaign proved unfruitful. All those dinners and parties I went to left me even more unloved than before, and made my intolerable loneliness more hopelessly unremedied by a mate. I had to dip into my reserve of self-pity by the bucketful; but the well turned up inexhaustible, replenished by a fund of tear ducts endowed by the rich, teeming resources of the earth's liquifaction. Thus came to be born a sort of natural piety of being unloved, or a private religious cult of cosmic everlasting consolation. This sophisticated itself into a doctrine of philosophical misery. Being unloved came to confer an elitist superiority, a divinely privileged solitude of the select. Exclusion from the lower blessings of the easy unconscious loved loving ones was not just exclusion from common earthly joy, but elevation to an *exclusive* rank: that of the loneliest of all, God. A mixed blessing, born of deprivation. But a majestic sublimation, nevertheless. Being unwanted, glorified above the "competition". Well out of the field of proven and repeated failures, but eminently out—from above.

But something pulled me down, dragged me back to earth. After having risen far above hope, I suddenly found myself in an amazing simplicity: I was loved and loving. A sordid comedown, in a sense; but, in all other senses, organically gratifying to my whole failure as a man. I had traded states—was I the better for the trade? Not better or worse, just different. Making more than a world of difference, between states not comparable. Spheres apart, in fact. But using my same mind, heart, and body, to outlast even the transformation itself, in a consistency undaunted by events. What is the nature of change? In what state is a man not himself? Through radical upheavals, the same man is lending his participation. Then what *does* matter? Fundamental happiness on the simple plane?; or compensatory consolation on a necessity-driven artificially constructed elevation of a sorrowed mind? Try them both out, try them all out—you're on trial. Life delights in what form it takes. Compressed into that form, squeezed and hedged into it, by zones of surrounding and converging suffering, that mold the man from all sides, into his refuge. A small island in his refuge, where his role is. His identity-social; his solace and salvation, privately. Away from; into. And once into, being. And being takes up living, in action. Life paused on its current phase.

SOME MINOR HISTORY

There was a party thrown for a political candidate, to raise funds in support of his campaign. The admission charge was quite a few dollars, but for that the paying guests received drinks and food, displayed on big tables, which they could just pick up and consume at will. Eventually, the political candidate vigorously waged his campaign backed by the funds raised at the fund-raising party. However, he failed to be nominated. So in retrospect, that party was only a fun-raising party. The food and drinks were successfully enjoyed, proving that not everything was a loss. The political candidate went into eclipse, and his projected career was abandoned. Instead, he continued with his career as a lawyer.

At the time of the party, there was such hope for him! Such optimism, with the food and drink!

More time has passed. The former political candidate, along with all his campaign promoters and party guests, have died. So now, what good was all that food and drink, even? It was all right for the *time*. But now . . .

JOSEPHINE'S LITERARY CHOICE

I

A student of contemporary literary criticism had stopped living some time ago, and had been reading instead. Like a swarm of locusts devouring a dry California plateau, she'd work her way through the *quality* contents of one branch library after another. The resources of her means of private finance were too slender to permit her to own so many books herself; but the central library and the university library, unlike branch libraries, were continually replenished and amply inexhaustible. Her goal, plodding through book after book, was to develop her critical and interpretive faculties and to apply them to every serious book ever written since the ancient discovery of words: but employing the sharp instruments of modern ways of evaluating all the dateless literary material. The most advanced standards were hers; she was thirty years old and wore glasses, had never been married, but caught the eye of the beholder as being uncommonly pretty when looked at in one way; or average passable when scrutinied the other. The "point of view" reveals the character.

Here it was, another Saturday evening, in the reading room of the almost oppressively omnipotent central library. She was being thirty years old and undated by any man that night; rather, all her gentleman escorts were the *authors* she was reading; almost all of whom were past their virile prime, being dead. It's hard to have a *personal* relationship with even a *handsome* dead man; even though he had been lionized, like the thrilling Lord Byron.

She stopped ruminating along literary lines long enough to take pause, sum up, take stock, and begin worrying: would she ever be a wife and mother? If so, she must hurry. Her prime was not getting riper. She had poured love into literature, as payment to purchase the art of mastering its scale of values for the purposes of being a connoisseur critic. But she had neglected her role as a *woman*. It wasn't too late. The alarm had been on time.

The warning is throbbing in her body. She must soon be mated. The right man would have to be found. She'd apply her hyper-literary taste to the more earthly plane of men, to choose indeed a worthy lover as the proper fit for her pride. She would not be sold short. A demigod would suit her fine, equal as a man to Dante, Goethe, or Cervantes as towering makers of word worlds. Her standards might be too exacting; but having laboriously acquired them, in painstaking remittance of toil, she was loath to lower them. She listed specifications that her prospective man would have to meet; should he fail them, he must be disqualified: just as certain authors—like Galsworthy, Maugham, Sinclair Lewis, E.E. Cummings, and Longfellow— simply didn't muster up. She had refined herself, and now at her just estimate and frank esteem, had no business to traffic with mediocrities in the literary realm or in her personal life. The test of character was to *enforce* the excellence of her acquired taste. As she spurned many authors as being comparatively unworthy, so, as a woman, she must do much rejecting before the right man became acceptable as her life's partner. She would exercise a rigor, in weeding out the candidates. Literature had taught her to be nobly exclusive—that is, excluding. She had perched a mentally lofty world for herself, which forbade most things to belong. Those that passed the test of belonging would *necessarily* have much to recommend them.

Great books were easily accessible, thanks to cheap modern type. But ranking *men* would have been snapped up and married by now, if they had the goods. On this score, she fell a-brooding, while Saturday night pounded away on the vast tables, stacked with opulent tomes, of the central library's hushed and velvety reading room.

Madame Bovary picked men from the romantic stereotype of books, and died in that martyrly cause. That example must be avoided. It would be stupid to parallel the good men to the good book. The standards were dissimilar; the present heroine of life, brooding late in the library, must recognize what a blunder it would be to equate the likely man with the masterful tome. She wouldn't beguile herself into the enchantment of a romantic trap on a literary basis, but would develop new criteria to separate men from literature, and by telling them apart, give both their full due of justice. This much was resolved. How to put it to practice, and to unbook herself of sentiments and notions of fancy and intellect peculiar to the bookish sphere of fictions and poetry, of drama and the essay; and to look full square at men, for what they are, divorced from the literary appraisal. This difficult transition, a phasing out from one quarter and an introduction to the other, needs be undergone, and now. Not a *translation* of one world by another; but learning a specifically different treatment. Such was her task. Thirty was a critical age. It prescribed recourses, however rash and desperate. The mastery of a new sphere of endeavor, like the learning of a new language, required submission to unfamiliar rules and an as yet foreign vocabulary; and a trial by new grammar.

What had happened to her as a girl from age fifteen to age thirty? Hadn't she put those years to *some* feminine account? Sure, so she wouldn't be starting from scratch, now. But how blinking novel is this outlook: like a mole that unburrows itself, startled by its first glare of the powerful sun, taken aback by rays so strangely un-underground. She must emerge from books, and be exposed to the rich torpor of sun and men. She'd rise into a woman's life: the more intense, for the background crawled up from. She'd be liberated *for* men, not *from* books. Not to sacrifice the latter; but to extol the former, as well.

From books, to graduate to men: from men, to *one* man: thus plotted her destiny, as closing time loomed up in the library's reading room. Her books in a pile before her, or strewn on the table in neglected stages of openness, spine up or spine down. She had thought through books, and her conclusion could be called "man." Her body had its biology to do; her heart needed companionship. She had done all that reading. She was mentally crammed with books. She was jammed with strategies of critical techniques for clustering the categories of books by their numerous cross-segmented designations; she was like Borges, or T.S. Eliot, or Dr. Johnson, in her extensive acquaintance with bodies of literature. Now, it was *life's* turn. When had she last had a *real* boyfriend? That was many books ago. She had measured out her life—in bookmarks! Now, the woman in her had put in a bid. An essential, basic demand by her own self-rooted cause. She would give it a womanly answer, by cramming it with man.

II

Scholars made their way out of the library. Josephine among them. She lightly trod toward her new life.

Having begun her dangerous decade of her thirties, she had almost belatedly managed to arm herself with her woman's destiny. Before which man should she dangle such a prize? Or where were there *any* men?

Her buoyancy became ponderous. It's nine o'clock of a Saturday night in the world's most colossal city, in winter's season of parties. She closed herself into a public telephone book, took out her notebook of phone numbers from her handbag that dangled from a shoulder strap, and with enough suitable coins at hand, began making a series of enquiries. One would be bound to work. A stray girl was always in demand.

On her fourth phone call, she connected with the right friends. They were a married couple, they were just off to a party, barely to the door before the phone call. They were so well invited, that it would be no problem for Josephine to accompany them. They gave her the party's address, and would meet her in front of the building, or in the lobby near the elevator. They'd get there before her, so Josephine should hurry and take a subway. A night of adventure was beginning to dawn. The future had unknown possibilities. It was close at hand. The party would be big, informal. No more delay by weighing what intriguingly lies before. Get down there, quick.

Bookish Josephine was riding on the subway. Could she read her way out into life, as she had read herself deep into books? Or would it make an awkward conversion—no, not conversion, but addition? She wouldn't renounce books. She'd develop the woman side of her, and continue to read.

Her life was undergoing an extension: not relinquishing her cultivated sharp critical touch in giving books their qualities; *keeping* that, but venturing out into a love life, as well. Could her system accommodate both? Why not?—they weren't mutually antagonistic: neither excluded either; they were non-prohibitive pursuits. They would be tethered together, in a joint enterprise.

III

The party was going on. A youngish university professor, bourbon glass held high in hand, with whisky bubbles popping out when he shook his wiry arm in intensity, had Josephine engaged in a topic not unfamiliar to her: books. The vigor of their exchanges gave a frothy *brio* of high heady dash to their well-shared conversation. In a minute, he looked ready to propose. They were falling down a deep, mutual, headlong tunnel. Their animation was diving swoon-deep, and their plunge would reach a pit of bed. They were a naturally amorous pair.

All the party guests who came as couples, remained so. All the ones who came singly, had now paired off. Especially Josephine, and her professor. They were sitting together deep back on a couch, with their persons in frank, unfurtive contact, from foot to head, all up and down his whole left side, and her right side. Alcohol made their period of being strangers exquisitively brief. Barely introduced, they were now half intimate. This was progress! The library meditation was bearing an instant fruition, practically. Visions of sex united them in anticipatory frenzy. They emitted pants, in unison.

What an easy non-transition, from being totally lonely, to being divinely merged! Suddenly, and complete.

Absolutely they made one. It was happening. It was foregone; and denial vanished, aghast!

Total romantic fusion. Each one had forgotten himself, in the willing loss that meant surrender to a whole—by which they were so snugly bound, into which they thrust their all. Had love any lower definition? Or had love higher to go? No, they and love made a trio. And the warbling had no end.

But suddenly she snapped to. Her individualism asserted itself. She was Josephine, not part of anything.

"Who are you? I don't even know your name."

"I told you before, but you were inattentive with bliss: I'm Bob. Is that an obstacle to our marriage?"

"Why precipitantly do you bring up such a premature subject? We've erected no foundation as yet, to make that an inevitable step. Being baseless, you soar off to heights, expecting me to accompany you on your flights of caprice, your drunken romantic whimsy sodden with lust. Come down, and quick! Your nerve is all presumption, headstrong, impetuous, unfounded. You expect my timing to coincide with your gliding?

Come down, right now! First learn of me, before you take liberties!"

IV

This chastening brought Bob up abruptly, and sobered him outright. How could she have spoiled it? It had been happening there between them; and then not! She had willfully halted it, in its immense stride. It had been sweeping them away, by momentum's full flight, to which they were held submissive as captives to the same happiness, together bound in one linked ecstasy. Now, she had shattered it! They had fallen into self-conscious parts. They were agonizingly separate. Overhead, and in front of them, the party blared forth. The other guests were now distinguished, that were a blur before. The couch they sat on was now their *arbitrary* link. What was nature's, now belonged to artifice. This sour wakening. By Josephine's sheer act of will. To prove her problematic freedom? To plunder the selfness of choice? By what law had she uglified their meeting into pure embarrassment bred by misadventure? In what strenuous perversity had she chanced to overcome a glorious rarity and undo a blessed accident? An uncommon destruction. To destroy an uncommon thing. Was too good a thing, too quickly come by, intolerable to her? Was bliss, by very intensity, unbearable as an utter stranger that had to be denied on impact? Bob wouldn't give up. He'd set Josephine the obligation of systematic explanation to account for her dastardly breaking of confidence and her rash conversion of doubly-bent innocence to the twin abyss of chasmic disaster on the ism of schism. He set an imperative on her apology. They would thrash this out, in a torture session. She wouldn't be let off lightly. She had provoked his devil, who would not be put off with appeasement. There would be thunder to pay. Josephine had provided an ordeal for herself; and Bob would vindictively hold her to it, till spasms of atonement come forth, and penance by mortification exacted. She toyed with a big thing, till it came apart; it would have to be paid for. She had to answer for what she destroyed. Bob packed her up in all her wintry effects and vehemently took his prisoner home: his, not hers. He'd drag insight from her captivity, and extract the most tortured confession. He'd bleed from her, book by book, all her drops of precious book-blood—it had to be shed. He'd drain her pale, look at the dregs, and tear from her his foremost conclusion on terms of white revenge, though her fainting might give a lethal signal in a white overspending of vitality's weakening reserve. Murder is meek, compared to what this murderer had done—she had murdered what was more precious than her bare self. Now her crime would be summoned, on their private trial. Only a personal justice can comply to a torn intimacy. What Bob was owed, was Josephine's to give.

V

They read book after book together. All was sweet restored harmony; she had in fact moved out of her own apartment and was living in his: well installed, along with his voluminous library. It was now the Easter vacation week away from university, so Bob's professional duties were relaxed and his devotion aided Josephine, whose studies had proliferated. She read at an alarming rate, and was far ahead of Bob who, for all his academic worth and his laureled prestige as a scholar, was no equal to Josephine's self-propelled genius. His ego was in conflict over this. As Josephine's lover, he had his pride to uphold. But he was easily outdistanced by her rapid consumption of books, which seemed like the progress of a disease: tuberculosis or some other wasting virus. Bob couldn't catch up with her; so the trick became, to slow her down.

How would she take his proposed rationing of her reading? Monomaniacally unwell.

"You won't interfere," she dictated. "We'll stop reading books together. I'll have my *own* reading life, independent of yours, and we'll each progress at rates apart, the way different trees or flowers do. Love is enough to share; love's principality is our meeting ground, and books would be redundant to it. We've joined our lives; but at this toll of compromise: let our minds have separate paths of development, as certainly mine does require. For you to entwine your restrictive ivy vine around my own advancing stem, to choke off its free growth and constrict my ever-promised flowering, would be the lover's crime that not even a court of love could condone. So let my mind go off, alone. Otherwise, I'll threaten to move out, and reluctantly add my *physical* independence to my insisted intellectual one. You won't head me off, for nature is determined in my high critical development; I'm beginning to write, and will produce major works to prove it. Don't let our emotions strangle my private mind. Set your pride aside, to grant me superior access, on a fertile field of solitude. Don't deny me this absolute, insisted condition; and the prize for your lenience, your side of the bargain, will be: you'll have me for a bride. Yet, don't construe this a bribe. Rejoice in my vaunted promise, and of your free joy, gladly give me pass; join, thus, your will to mine. And you'll be a major critic's husband. And I'll be: a dull professor's wife. If you're agreed, let's kiss and do more: and disrobe. We'll have a bouncing bed for our common ground; while my larger brain will do its divine hunting, remote from your smaller-sized one. Respect this division, not as an insult, but as nature's rugged and uneven law. Where there's no equality, I'll romp, while you'll slide. Show your big-souled acceptance of your lesser role, and nobly endure it. I'm the family's prodigy; while your level must hold on evenly to its mediocre allotment. This is not intended, but observed; and for our better life together, to be obeyed. Now, let's make love: just to prove that you're not entirely emasculated. Pardon my ascendency, in our natural comparison. In return, I'll grant you superior masculinity. Prove it, and pin me down, please."

VI

They were married in the marrying month of June. Bob let her live her own life, and took revenge, for being slighted, by sporadic infidelities with some girlish members of the student body and willing women faculty members. Josephine, as all the while predicted, rose to eminence as a major and often-quoted critic whose brilliance and fair-mindedness were of legendary dimensions: she was reputed to be Coleridge's equal, and Hazlitt's superior, in their chosen fields of letters. Honorary degrees were conferred on her by the vying universities, with Bob's being no exception. Bob closed his jealousy in secrecy, and plotted a more gruesome revenge than his clandestine adulteries. Josephine would have to be dishonored; to this profound end, Bob brought all his powers together, to evilly conspire. Josephine's downfall, her sordid disgrace, were being schemed. Bob was a laughingstock, for being the plodding consort of the reigning queen of the intellect. This was not to be borne lightly; he gathered his dark malice, and invoked devil-borrowed powers, to inspire a superb revenge to end Josephine as a threat. He must weaken her brain, to damage it beyond repair. That would enfeeble her faculties, she'd stop writing, her career would stop; her addiction to books would be forever paused. Till then, Bob couldn't rest. To resort to so foul a thing, to fell and arrest the too-endowed Josephine! To put a woman . . . in her place. This was to earn all men's gratitude, who had to endure superior loved ones. Thus Bob felt justified for his fallen deed.

VII

"It's righteous of me," he monologued one night. Josephine was in her study, finishing a critical masterpiece comparing all periods of literature with each other in terms of the prevailing conditions historical to their given societies; and she showed how civilized culture is molded by works of art, as well as reflected. This would revolutionize the study of history, literature, all of art, civilization, society, and culture. What an ambitious book to be written! It was her fame's prancing pinnacle, and on such an opus her already solid reputation would be so firmly established, so imperishably entrenched, that her universal significance would last forever as America's premier contribution to man as a reading animal. So too, monumentalized, would bristle the abstract of all masculine jealousy on Bob's suffering head. Thus darkened this husband's brooding to find a form of adversity of firmest ruin to so intellectual a wife and enemy. A fiend's agony wouldn't be enough. Perfection would have to breed a total harm to unsoar in full flight a woman paragon's exaltation of language and concept. Was it loo big for destruction to undermine? Then boost destruction into a bigger might for this titanic accomplishment. The honor of all men, in every age, was the stake Bob would fight for, in bringing down this mere woman who simply did not know her place. Men have domination over the mind: Bob would enforce this.

Unaware of such unhusbandly intentions, Josephine was alternately writing and typing, to complete her crowning work. Her publisher was greedy for the manuscript. He had halted all other printing schedules, to prepare for this unprecedented priority. He would be arriving next morning in a taxi, with a metal suitcase with a lock, to take her typewritten pages in the sanctity of foolproof safekeeping. And he would have two armed escorts with him; the police had granted him this civil license, in this solemn wedding of an immense business break-through (of boon to the whole publishing enterprise on a huge economic scale) with a cultural event whose implications were of greater stupendor than the moon's American rape.

Well, Bob wasn't going to sit back and let it happen. He'd put an end to the myth of the passive male in America. His act would be of interference. To sabotage a woman's greatness would be the elevation of his whole gender, in this pronounced case. Bob and Josephine were symbols: the game at stake was the whole sexual race. To reaffirm man's primacy, was Bob's greater role.

To strike a woman off her high saddle, and land her back in her lowly functions of housekeeper, cook, and birthgiver, and sexual object and child tender. To strike for all reactionary grass roots, and return mankind to basics. To kill off the "women's liberation" campaign, so popular among radicals today.

Bob was a martyr in a cause of such sweep. He must pluck the head out of Josephine—if necessary by burning her manuscript to enrage her into madness and provoke her to a crime that all women would be punished for. To earn history's approbation for men, and her eternal condemnation of women, who would be struck from glory on the strength of Josephine's flop, her archangel-like fall from a false and literary grace. To restore some semblance of sanity, with men at rule.

VIII

Bob was determined to die, but Josephine would have to kill him. She'd value her manuscript, so he'd burn it. In her fury . . . Well, Bob would pay. But so would Josephine.

In the end, man would rise to regain his lead, in his eternal tussle with women for supremacy. Bob would historically redeem the balance, by making a villain of Josephine, with himself in the martyr role. But to be a martyr, he must make it seem that he did not burn the manuscript. He would have to plant the guilt on Josephine's head, while himself incurring her homicidal wrath. A difficult prize: necessity would have to battle for it. By one stroke or self-sacrificial cunning, Bob would overcome the cultivated life time of Josephine's flowering genius. That would even up those odds that mocked him so, in his outranked subjugation to a wife's eloquent erudition. The lowly must resort to tricks across the unflattering talent gap. Democracy upheld with poster idealism the brute jungle tactics that would blunt the refined and coarsen all edges. Equality advertised its justification, on any ground.

By luck, the telephone rang; a literary colleague of Josephine was calling, so she left her study to where the phone was waiting two rooms away. Bob prayed that the phone talk would be long-winded. Such a prospect would arm his opportunity with its crucially strengthened time. He crept into her study. But this was a modern apartment, and there was no fireplace. So he'd heat the oven and roast her pages there. He gathered up her extensive manuscript, minus an overflowing page or two, and cradled the bulging pack in both arms under his tickled chin. But she always made carbon copies! Laden with his burden, he searched for the carbon-copy manuscript. There it was, on an adjoining desk. What a time to get caught red-handed! He heaped the copy-manuscript onto the original, and staggered with an awkward load, to whose bulky mastery he felt frantically weakened, in a critical time. He wasn't cut out for crime. And he was caught. His wife returned, The phone call had been brief.

"An instinct of survival made me cut short that important call. I had a premonition that your jealousy was up to something desperate, and would employ any ruse, even this very legitimate and unstaged phone summons, to expedite your dirty work afoot. Here's a hysterical proposition for you. I caught you flat-footed, and look how foolish you are, trembling red-veined under a wife's envied product. I have one recourse: to divorce you."

Bob relieved himself by replacing the manuscript on the desks, both copies back in their proper place, like an abashed but dutiful son obediently atoning for surreptitious offense which the parent condescended to notice. "You have the upper hand, I think," was Bob's rejoinder. Josephine would have to dispatch the case quickly, mercifully or not, according to an expedient verdict that would get her back to her desk to add the finishing touches to a work of far greater weight than her simpleton husband. The publisher would taxi-arrive by the morning, with his expensive precautions of ceremonious practicality. It must be ready by then for him. First, to get rid of Bob, and disarm him morally, to reduce his will against another attempt of final treachery to a spouse. He was so easy to detect, but it was time-consuming, and emotionally taxing. How could she placate his envy? The man needed reassuring. His male vanity— could she restore it? How could she seem weak? She must beguile him into an illusion of his power. She must appeal to his pity, by deceptively arousing his protective might. But this was impossible. She, a published author, he, a puny professor! The obvious odds were stacked in her impressive favor.

IX

"No more mischief, please. If I catch you at such another bungled undermining of me, my work, my career, I'm going to have you locked up, for I'm friends with the police chief, who's a literary buff in his spare time. I know what you're up to. Can you cut it out? If not, a jail sentence will ruin your university tenure prospects, and eliminate all your academic ambitions to one day rise to dean or to the departmental chair. How would you like that, dear?"

"I stand chastised, and if you'll only cease intimidating me—which is so very easy for you to do—I vow never to obstruct your greatness or impede the strides of your genius in the triumphs of bearing publishing fruit. I'll take a back seat, to your foremost rank in our marital inequality. But may I suggest . . . a pride-restoring compromise?"

"I'm busy, so be brief. What is it?"

"Let's produce a child. Let's take off our contraceptive devices, which we've been careful to keep on till now, to allow your industrious enterprise and prolific literary purpose to prosper. Can't you extend your fertility to motherhood as well? For then our child would have your brilliance, but my vanity. And I could identify with your superiority through the vehicle of our *common meeting ground*: the child we will both share. In our joint ownership, I'll be reconciled to my lesser importance. Our essences will be merged, in the same child, as a symbolic union. Then I'll recognize your greatness, accord you its privilege, with no bitter envy. I'll love you as you are: and encourage you to work even harder as the critical lioness of our day, to accumulate a truly prodigal authorship. Our bloodstreams will be mingled in our baby, your genius with my mediocrity. I'll then be a part of you, through the kid. That will redeem my faith in myself, and make my manhood less shaky when linked with your mental dominance through the biological equalizer that levels power out evenly and allots the greater share to the lesser, in a balance appeasing to my vanity, rendering my homicidal hostility against you harmless and redundant by eliminating a bitter cause in an overall blend of love and family. Our differences won't matter, then. It'll work very well for me. Your output will be acceptable, and not a challenge. By vanquishing the threat, I'll be your toothless spouse, paternally your equal, by love's family institution. And it will save our marriage. Can you match this plan with your consent, on an equal footing of wills? I offer you unvying love, and will bar competition as a plane of masculine strife. That will ease life for you, and your leisure will go on, unabated—but consolidated maritally, having been given my conjugal blessing—to create ever excellent works of criticism. It's good for you, it's good for me, this plan. What do you say?"

"It would work, except that I've stopped loving you. My work is foremost, and you've receded dreadfully, till my life can find no consequence in you. I resolve to rid myself of you and call it quits. Until then, my freedom couldn't be called my own. Be understanding and see my point of view. You won't stand in my way, once you find it my better welfare to be devoid of your company. I yearn for the old solitude, minus you. Now I want to return to work. The morning will soon bring my publisher. That's so much more urgent than you. You always come last in the priority stakes. This drains your vanity away, with the rage to compensate emboldened to criminal fury. You're well rid of me. I'll abjure you. Shut the door, behind you. Tomorrow we'll part. It's the only way, in all full dignity. Your pride is low when you live with me. Released to freedom, you'll gain your steady level, and pursue your best life, without competitive interference. Accept our oncoming divorce. It must be, perforce."

X

She was locked in her room, working. Bob was outcast. His exile had been announced, and the matter closed shut. He had an abandoned soul to nurse: his own, alas.

Bob was staggered, and wept. Her declaration of rejection carved a brutal finish on his total humiliation and polished the abuse of his ego to an extent he could never recover from. Josephine had administered the *coup de grace*, by ruthlessly turning down his domestic rescue suggestion that would patch up their differences. The hour was eerily late. He had a morbid night.

He could but submit. To ponder anything else would be futile. Her will had been made clear. He was too passive now for hate and murder. He had been drained of violence. Numbness and repose were the peaceful remedies, for fury had shown itself impotent. He would humbly absorb this defeat. The trial was at an end. How could Josephine be opposed? He would worship that majestic queen. From afar. His role would be: her former husband. It would calm his dignity and weigh his solace over with tragedy's dramatic balm. To be the toppled consort, to live out his days in philosophy's pale glamor over a meditative soul. To sink away, serenely. To leave Josephine alone, but claim her in enshrined memory, the inaccessible he had once laid claim to, before mystic renunciation took his pride away, eased his manhood out, and left him in romantic reverie. Ah, what a sweet thing. To be lessened into glory. And to will the soul away.

He was asleep at dawn. Josephine had finished her work. She found him, sleeping benignly, sitting slouched on an armchair. She knew she had won. She was hers, alone. But by work, it was to the world she belonged. Fame had commended her. Soon the doorbell would ring. Her devout publisher would appear. He would ease her of her product. And she would gain renown. Renown was hers already. She served literature. She had more to give.

PARTY CRASHING

HOW TO FAIL AT CRASHING A PARTY

To crash a party, first
don't be acquainted with the host.
Furtively wait outside,
not directly in front
of the conspicuous entrance.
And when the invited guests
start arriving in little clusters
or even pairs,
sidle in with them
as though belonging but invisible,
deftly maneuvering
as though you're a genuine invitee
knowing you haven't come for a cup of tea.
Others may bring bottles but it's not mandatory
under formal obligation
to make a casual contribution,
nor your identity have an attribution.
Dress like the others do
so you won't be ejected at the door
if someone confronts you with a list
of welcome guests without your name,
and you're exposed to your shame.
Protest that this isn't a police state
under stern dictatorship
of "in" people and you're out,
marginal, by the wayside,
lonely, unpartnered,
outside, longing for true love
and soaking in your self-pitying solitude.
The party is there but you can't intrude.
Just an isolated interlude
of feeling unbelonging.

You're barred, despite your lonely longing.
Your mouth is dry. You're not in the mood for songing.
"Poor myself!" you inwardly exclaim,
as a would-be party guest:
so deprived, you pretend it was all in jest.
Having failed, at least you tried your best.

NOT BEING A PROBLEM AS AN UNCOUTH PARTY-CRASHER

A collusion between host and guest
at a party requires you do your best
to be worth your place though you crashed the party
uninvited but you squirmed your way in
and now prove that you really fit,
and make your host's approval
so high as not to demand your removal.
Then you can eat all the food you want
and get drunk too at the liquor font,
but furtively by piece-by-piece
so as not to disturb the real guests' peace
and proficiently provide for their ease
so that your barrage of manners is bound to please
by not being a hog nor a free-loader
too conspicuously as to set you apart
to glare out that your host's party is not smart.
Then if you get drunk you have to stay
and not go home, to your host's dismay.
This farce is worthy of a Broadway play.

**ISABEL (THE HOSTESS) VERSUS THE RAIN'S TIMING
JUST AS SHE WAS PRIMING FOR A VERY PLANNED PICNIC
ON WHICH THE RAIN DECIDED TO PICK.
THAT DECISION WASN'T WORTH A LICK.**

The rained-on picnic is an obstacle
to good timing. Isn't it possible
for the rains to reserve an appropriate time
—but not a picnic—to come on strong?
By coincidence, the rain was wrong
to spray its deep wet song
on that planned and particular picnic
that it just happened, on the spot, to pick.
I would call this coincidence "sick."
Also the hostess: She was so miserable
that she (her name is Isabel)
wrote an apology letter to her guests
vindicating herself: she had tried her best
not to schedule that horrid rainfest
on a deplorable rainy day
with blankets spread on the grass.
And on the blankets, food and wine.
No wonder afterward she was heard to whine.
Couldn't the weather have decently turned out fine?
What bad luck it happened to be
that the timing upset the schedule with misery,
and what "could have been" wandered away, free
for the angry mind to contemplate.
A real social event! Well, that's fate.
Isabel (the hostess)
was just a rainstorm away from being the mostest.
Instead, she accused herself of being the grossest,
but decided to make the rain the scapegoat,
pinning the awful blame
on the arbitrary fluke of the game.

But still, isn't it lame
to cast any cowardly blame?
She may only cause her gut to inflame.

**I CRASH A MEMORIAL PARTY
FOR SOME DEAD SUCKER I DON'T KNOW
AND PUT A STRANGER'S DISGRACE ON IT
AND CAN NEVER SHOW MY FACE THERE AGAIN
FOR WHATEVER NEXT DEAD PERSON
HER FAMILY PAYS TO MOURN THERE
AND WASTE A LOT OF EMPTY FUNERAL AIR.**

Someone died, and his friends made ceremony.
It was all based on what's phony.
There's nothing left of him, so why celebrate?
Exploit the ceremony, there's free food and drink.
Also you could meet someone for sex in the future
that could even lead to marriage,
and even yet, to a baby carriage.
Plus, you could gossip about the dead one,
get drunk, and have great conversations,
sprinkled with more humor than you know how to use.
If you feel mean, you can demean
the party's celebrant with foul abuse,
taking a risk with such insults
to make the real guests be mad at you
even to the point of asking you to leave,
since you haven't shown the decency to bereave.
So what? You drunkenly weave your way out,
having inflicted on the dead one dishonored flout,
and yourself a son-of-a-bitch reputation.
He's dead, so what's this bother anyway?

We're not stupid believers as to kneel and pray.
To hell with him—but there's no hell,
so what the hell? I feel nice and swell.
For what dead sucker is that funeral bell
that irrelevantly sounds with an empty knell?

**THE UNCERTAINTY PATTERN
IF YOU TRY TO FIGURE IT OUT,
BUT THE WHOLE PLAN EXPLODES IN A SUDDEN ROUT
AND YOU INWARDLY FIND YOURSELF ON THE OUT.
SUDDENLY ALL CONFORMS
INTO A BUNCH OF NEW NORMS.**

Try living, and you get an odd mixture
whereby variety is your only fixture
and the results are entirely uneven,
and expectation is met with surprise.
Even trying to live in eternity's sunrise
gets slapped in the face as reality intervenes
when the unusual comes inbetween
foregone conclusions anticipated
but intercepted by the unexpected.
All the odds are out of the window
when warm weather is overturned by snow,
emphasizing the adage, "you'll never know,"
confusing deep-laid plans where to go
and you're in a state of sudden vertigo.
So let's all go to a party
where the hostess faints at the sight of you,
where the grotesque and the mild will intermix
and you whisk right through being in a fix.
That's life, with its open bundle of hidden tricks.

You really knew what was coming
till it exploded into the unbecoming,
and previous laws are of no use,
adding rigid confusion to brisk plans
to settle down on a new leaf
till you implode at the latest disbelief.
Life explores, then retracts, its agonized relief.
Uncertainty is the code we know
when the winds of coincidence decide to blow.

MY FAVORITE PARTY

An Essay That Never Got Written

If I had to write an essay entitled, "My Favorite Party," I would first try to remember which were my favorite parties; I would shorten the list by eliminating the less-than-the-best of the parties that I honor with the distinction of considering them on my list of all-time remembered favorites.

Of course, memory is renowned for playing tricks. Something remembered, whether a party, a picnic, a love affair, a job, a school class, a no-longer-seen friend, a former anything, becomes a *remembered* event, and is experienced as a *memory*. Of course, remembering can bear crucial ties to the way those remembered things earlier were actually experienced in those former times: when one was undergoing for the first time—on the spot—the initial raw material to be later distilled, converted, translated, transformed, transmuted, transcended, into—as it were—the stuff of memory (including that bittersweet, emotionally laden phenomenon known as nostalgia, accompanied subtly on the violin in poignant reminder).

Through the process of elimination, I've now narrowed down the short list of potential candidates for "My Favorite Party" (as the title of the projected essay goes, with the text itself to be placed beneath, in the neatness of their sequence, as the order of the writing will dictate) to four hundred or a little more. This of course, keeps my memory ferociously active: like a single bee drunkenly darting from flower to flower in a profuse meadow of a June botanical spectacular, gathering this one's pollen and that one's pollen, reelingly careening in a spree or binge with increasingly heavy a load of a burden of a weighing-down of its corporeal little bee-body in its buzzing hum of bee-like busy-being; with promiscuous pollen-acquisition, in greedy collecting-industry of gorging pick-up rounds in dizzy dives here, dizzy dives there, dripping pollen, oozing in the stuff, but stoking the bulk away, in storage for the flowerlessly out-of-season session of "a rainy day." (If it's not already dead by then, poor bee, so short is the pitiable brief reign of its slight life-span, though the species drones on in its collectively eternal life, through the generations of its ever-dying members considered each as an individual tragedy from our too-human point of view.)

However, I digress from parties—or rather, their memory—or rather, *my* memory of them (the parties that I *attended*, that is—not, certainly, the ones I didn't).

I've now reduced my short-list of candidates for "My Favorite Party" to less than four hundred, which I'll carefully cull and go over with a fine-tooth comb to separate "superlative" from "merely great"; as the ruthless process of elimination continues with the dredging of memory's gems from the treasure-laden depths of experience's old sea-bottoms, where sunken galleons send up shimmering ghosts of invaluable recollections from the precious bowels of dust-rusted, water-logged, fish-strewn, bubble-popping cargo remnants, twisted out of recognition into the "rich and strange" that underwent "a sea change."

Yes, but what about the parties themselves?—before successions of memories diluted, distorted, exaggerated, contorted them with selections, emphases, composites, linking, merging, romanticizing, shame-repressions, inaccuracies, confusion, and partial forgetfulness over time's grossly inefficient network of filing disorder and musty records chaotically kept in ruined archives of neglect?

"My Favorite Party"? No. I have no single favorite. None sticks out as being heads and shoulders in obvious superiority by some measured scale above its worthy competitors.

Parties are memorable for different reasons. This one for its serenity, that for ecstatic abandon; this for intellectual conver-

sational content, that for the briskness and ease of flirtational-
ity; this for useful career recommendations, contacts, connections, practical "operating," wheeling-dealing, later to be gratefully drawn upon; that for the magnificent buffet, its gourmet
spread; this for wonderful drinking hallucinations; that for its
entertainment and dancing; this for great guest-rapport in a
glow of mutual fondnesses as the germs for later friendships;
that for its sizzling erotic impact.

By leaving ever unwritten "My Favorite Party," I sensitively
spare the feelings and claims of all the fine parties that would
otherwise find themselves excluded from being the prizewin-
ning subject to which the title of the unwritten essay unmistak-
ably alludes. Why offend so many delicate feelings?—the special parties whose good will I retain to keep them potentially
fresh in the pickled jar of vivid recalling. The rejected contes-
tants for the signal honor could, in hurt spite, in huffing pride,
withdraw their brilliant former essences from the parlor or forum of sweet recollection, and leave me bereft and abandoned,
impoverished: as spurned goddesses may punish the contest
judge who awarded the prize apple to a detested other.

Let, periodically, all prized parties be cleanly aired in the
hallowed chambers of my memory for their assorted variegated
distinctive qualities and virtues. Some parties belatedly seek
admission after long immersions in hibernation confines, dor-
mantly keeping breath alive till they presently arrive wanting
sustenance and entertainment in the loyal faculties kept in
readiness in hospitable succor for those friendly relics emerged
shrouded from the foggy webs of their reticence submerged
in caverns below the welcome greeting level of consciousness
turned retrospectively back.

The decision never to write "My Favorite Party" is justly celebrated by that lethargic duo, Idleness and Indolence. They
bask in relief, and languidly toast their last-minute reprieve

with hearty drinks whose alcoholic content helps recall innumerable parties spread throughout the multi-layered temporal strata from Past Distant to Past Recent: those cluttered events drawn together in time's curious warp, while overlapping in condensed inaccuracies that borrow each other's features in free exchanges or weirdly motley combinings. No party remains strictly in its "place." They dart about, like cells in protoplasmic random square-dance orgies. These parties are never still. They have easily irritable membranes. They have my whole mind to share, like hordes of restless children with an enormous school yard to play about in: games bisect with other games, as the children are flung about in discipline's laxity, hurled dizzy on the shifting planes of wild freedom continually expanding across borders, margins, and boundaries in freely interchanged combinational novelties, generating perpetual flow, interflow, in the ranging flux of ongoingness's compounding expressions from earlier basic immutable elements.

If all the parties I ever attended were just one big party—why—what a party that would be! Just to contemplate it gives me a fit of staggers.

All the world's a party. Or rather, an apartment. And in that apartment, Life (the party) takes place.

Wrong. All the world's many party sites; containing, in turn, one by one, life's party series: which memory is always mixing up, with its liberal talent for transfusional confusion.

(Postscript:) Anyone who wanted to read the serious account of "My Favorite Party" is free to find solace in writing it himself. With that, I release my burden.

MARVIN COHEN VISITS FRED GUTZEIT IN HIS STUDIO

FG: Marvin, thanks for stopping by for a studio visit.

MC: Oh yeh!

FG: I know you've been around, you're a writer and playwright but you've been interested in art and know artists and been to a lot of exhibitions and familiar with artists' work.

MC: Boy do I like exper—expeditions—no: *exhibitions*. But sometimes I'm very indiscriminate because I want free—um—wine; red wine, but if there's only yellow wine; that's not as healthy as red wine. But the idea, of course, is for me to go to openings because I was born poor and grew up poor and so I figure that anything that I can get free so I exploit art.

But art is important in its own case, so sometimes in the case in the case of friends, like you!, I really look at their art and then I see that there is a lot to appreciate but in general I have a philistine approach to—um—openings, I want to talk to people, mainly to say hello to the people I've already known and we haven't made any appointment. So I guess they're not friends. Or maybe they are friends but a definition of a friend is somebody you've made an appointment with—so if I casually bump into somebody that's accidental and that may be the only way that I see that person. We're glad, maybe, because there's no commitment, we didn't make an appointment by phone or something like that.

So anyway; art—woo, boy do I like art! And then when I was in England, so Francis Bacon; I knew him and he was a celebrity. So I was so awed to know that celebrity—and I felt then that I thought; boy could I name-drop, wow! So I tried to see him as much as possible until I became so obnoxious that he said—

um—make it less frequent. So I'd go to his studio—oh there'd be dinner parties and so forth, he was a good cook. And he liked to gamble but the gambling part of his life, he put on a tuxedo and he went to fancy places; kind of night clubs and—he kept that apart, compartmentally from his artwork. And his artwork, he didn't say anything about it. And I saw that he covered his canvasses in his studio and he seemed to have gone through a lot of destruction of his previous canvasses. And in generally he seemed to be a person who destroys himself because he liked rough trade when it came to homosexuality. A lot of his friends, like me, were not homosexual—but he had this hidden life, and he would kind of take chances, and the chances he took were similar to—the chances he took in his canvas. You'd figure that he'd get into a pattern—so where he could handle it all right. Taking chances is going away from what you can handle.

Anyway, as far as life goes; I'm getting old, and I'm scared of dying. When people ask me: "how are you?" it's such a conventional question, it doesn't mean anything. You're supposed to say: "I'm very well, thank you. How are you?" and then "I'm very, how are you?" And so it goes back and forth, like a stale yoyo, or a stale ping-pong. But anyway, because I'm getting so old, I'm afraid that my life, will get unhealthy, which happens in old age. I feel all these obituaries, and it scares me because a lot of those people who die enough so that they can get in the obituaries—of course they have to be enough well known, because obituaries can't cover everybody—they're younger than me! They're dead and they're younger than me! What am I doing with extra life?

I'm a survivor,—ooh—I appreciate this extra life. Just like if I butt into a dinner and I freeload a dinner out of somebody, I try to eat as much as I can. The third helping, I try to eat before second helping because I figure the host is courteous enough to give me a second helping—and so if I take the *third* helping *first* he's so polite that he'll give me the second helping anyway—because that's the nature of his generosity. But his generosity stops short at the third helping. So first, I help myself to the helping. *[laughs gleefully]*

But anyway, I have an appointment—no, no, no—not for death but I have an appointment to go! Very nice to see you Fred. Nice to see you, so long!

FG: Marvin, thanks for stopping by.

[Note: transcript of July 2012 video: https://vimeo.com/45805052]

MARVIN COHEN'S SURREALIST HUMOR

by Justine de Lacy
from the *International Herald Tribune*, September 6/7 1980

LONDON—Marvin Cohen was having one of his more fruitful London summers. Lolling in the garden of a count's three-story house in Chelsea last week, he reflected on this as he sipped the count's Chablis.

Marvin was taking care of the count's objects for the second summer in a row. (Marvin doesn't take objects seriously, but be understands that other people do.)

He had not always been so lucky. There were the days of small hotels, attic rooms scrounged here and there. But that was before he was published and adopted by some of the more playful English well-to-do.

Now he stays in their houses when they are there, as well as when they are away, feeds their cats and eats their escargots. People of note give dinner parties for him. Daughters of Cabinet ministers phone. ("They love me in London," says Marvin, who is from New York. "I have the English eating right out of my hand.")

Marvin is cherished because he keeps people from being bored. People will go a long way for someone who keeps them from being bored.

Marvin doesn't let it go to his head. ("They roll out the red carpet because I'm only here two months a year and I don't wear holes in the welcome, if you know what I mean.") Listening to Marvin is like hearing the Bald Soprano recite Lewis Carroll during a performance of *Endgame*.

Writer, amateur surrealist, housesitter and partygoer extraordinaire, Marvin has had stories and parables in 85 publications and published eight books, including several collections of short fiction, *Fables at Life's Expense*, *The Inconvenience of Living, The Self-Devoted Friend, Others, Including, Morstive Stern-bump*, a novel, and a book of baseball essays. Marvin loves baseball. ("I like the drama of a tussle," he explains.) A story appeared in The New York Times that concerns a cockroach who went to a PR firm to have its image changed.

Marvin is not without his fans. Buckminster Fuller: "Morstive Sternbump's philosophy is congruent with my own." Thomas Merton: "His books should be read immediately by all who gladly recognize themselves to be half crazy." The New York Times Book Review: "What Mr. Cohen has is his own: a joy in language and an eye, at once innocent and shrewd for the paradoxes inherent in the human condition. He puts both language and people through their paces, stands them on their heads and hugs them to his heart . . ."

Now, however, Marvin is "frustrated, stifled and stymied by the world publishing crisis recession," and has turned to the theater. His *Don Juan and the Non-Don Juan,* a series of cabaret skits produced at the Public Theater last March, is being put on here at the National Poetry Society Centre, London SW5, beginning on Sept 9. The characters include "a nunhood-renouncing nun, a monthly duo named May and June, a rich gangster's smitten wife and a flowery trio named Iris, Rose and Lila."

"It's about the love seesaw. I love you then you love me a little less but oh now your love for me is fading so I love, *love* you and it's killing me. Poor me. I'm *dying* of love!"

Marvin wrote a play about Don Juan because he believes in love: "We must love passionately—alcohol, playing cards, air balloons, women, nature, furniture, God or whatever." (The invitation to a publishing party for one of Marvin's books starts "Dear Madam or whatever.")

He is pro-hilarity and anti-mortality. "I think mortality is the very worst thing about life. I'm against it, on my behalf and on that of others." Marvin hates cynics. "I like to be with bright people who aren't cynical. Life has a lot of possibilities of good-ness and pleasure. I don't want to be deprived of this by clever cynical minds." He grins. "*Or* by un-clever cynical minds."

On occasion, "if there's free food and drink," Marvin will tolerate bores. "Usually I eschew egocentrics, unless their ego-centricity is compensated for by sufficient glittering. Narcis-sists must earn their keep."

It has been two years now since Marvin has had a book pub-lished, and he admits he is getting discouraged. "I used to write with a glowing fervid warm coal of a hope expectation that I'd be in print and reach people's minds. Now I have a sort of de-spair."

"I need ears. I want to reach out, but not, of course, like the Ancient Mariner who would grab you by your lapel and act like an albatross on you." He grins. "What I'd like is for my ideas not to live and die in my own head but strike some kindred chord. I want to make a bridge. Love is one way. Art and literature are another. They allow you make a bridge to multiple minds, if you're lucky to collective minds. But the publishers' are not co-operating."

Basically, the London Marvin—of Kensington, Chelsea and Brompton Square—and the New York Marvin—of Seventh Street on the Lower East Side—do the same things: Read, write, reflect and go to parties. "Parties are my ballpark, my arena, my Coli-seum, my stock market and my social parachute jump. A party means an alarm is going off in the social beehive. Lives criss-crossing. I like to dissect the lives that bisect."

In the old days, Marvin indulged in "promiscuous partygoing—crashing, if you will." But now, at 49, he only crashes "maybe eight or nine parties a year." "Now that I'm hon-orably published, I'm invited a lot." Jasper Johns once came to lunch. ("I gave him a napkin made out of wax paper. It wasn't very absorbent. He was a bit disappointed, I'm afraid.")

It was rumored that Marvin used to go to New York parties wearing a bathing cap. "They mean my aviator's hat with the flaps my mother made me to keep the rain from getting in my ear. Anyhow, I only wore it to the party, not inside."

Marvin is partly deaf, the result of double mastoiditis when he was 3. He wears a hearing aid, which he switches off when bored. "Some people say I'm eccentric, but a lot of that is because I can't hear."

As a child, he never really felt "part and parcel" of the human community, he says. "I was out of rhythm, out of step. I didn't dance or anything and I couldn't learn. I was a loner. I didn't want to be left out but people weren't exactly jumping all over themselves to include me in. Some loners have to carry shopping bags around just to hold on to some thing of the world. Bag ladies and so forth. Of course, I'm a mild case compared to them."

Marvin began going to parties out of loneliness. "I never really starved, but I had a lonely soul. I wanted love. I wanted love! I wanted love *forever*! I felt uncompoundable. Parties were my only consolation. The process of writing is hermetic, a William Blake cocoon, a self-regenerated insulated universe. It creates a terrible longing for companionship."

Marvin has never owned a ring or a watch. ("Basically he doesn't believe in time." a friend says, though he's never late.) He likes to wear "grays and quiet plaids, anonymity coloration." His clothes come mainly from thrift shops. Marvin explains: "I've had a life of having to make my own way with no money, nothing from my parents and hating to work."

Marvin has had more than 150 odd jobs—mink farmer to merchant seaman—but was often fired for writing on the job. ("My non-commitment to the interests of the firm was often too readily recognized by the proprietor of the firm.") Today he teaches writing part-time at various New York universities.

He has a girlfriend, so he is not lonely anymore, but he still goes to parties "for people." What has been written about Morstive is equally true of Marvin: "Others are his study . . . at once his aggravation and his love . . ."

"Parties are my library," Marvin explains. "The living gallery of humanity interests me more than any collection of books. I'd rather talk to people than read books. One person is worth a thousand pages. That's why I go to parties, not because I'm a silly social butterfly on the make.

"While I'm here, I want to feel ties with my fellow men. In that way I'm like Walt Whitman! And Wordsworth! But Wordsworth was more of a hermit kind of guy. He didn't care for parties. He just liked natural things. Whitman and I consider socializing gregariously as steeping ourselves inside the pulse and throb and beat of multiple nature, all these people with their faces, their clothing."

Marvin enjoys "the semi-strife of social life, the rough and tumble and knocking about. I like to romp in the wildness and mystery of parties. They often bring out the pith and essence of people. You can divide up the sheep from the goats and so forth under the certain strenuous relaxed urgency that parties provide. Some nice people turn lousy, some rotten people turn nice."

This is even true of Marvin: "Sometimes, amid the beaming palsy-walsy of a party, there's a nice Marvinsparkle that shows up. But in the presence of aggressive, hostile flack, bad Marvinisms often come out.

"I go to parties, too, because I need solitude." Huh? "At parties you get your dose of people all in a lump. I prefer a smorgasbord in the evening to semi-snacking all day long."

Marvin also goes to parties to gather language. He is a master of the mixed metaphor—"the mixmaster metaphor, if you will"—sultan of seductive sententiousness, titan of tautology.

His hearing problem partly accounts for his Nabokovian ear for the rhythms of speech. ("I have a good ear because I have a bad ear and I have to listen twice as hard.")

At parties, he sits in the center of the room like a snapping turtle on a rock, waiting for tidbits of dialogue he can internalize and use to make more Marvin. "I fill myself with the matrix and fabric of human voices in the yapping cacophony of social intercourse. Many voices merge into my muse. Thousands of thous."

The thing Marvin really can't stand, in addition to "loud electronic music," is trivia: "What people ate, where they went, politics, economics, the weather, the stock market, where they buy their dog food, their clothes. There has to be an idea behind it or I don't have time."

These days, he goes to parties to look for a marketplace for his work. "I'm a one-man business, self-employed entrepreneur for very little money, and the world has not exactly fallen all over itself to break a beaten path to my door, if you know what I mean. I sorta have to kick a few people in the shins."

But Marvin is not discouraged. "To hell with the publishers. I'll keep submitting what I've written, and if they keep rejecting it, that's all right because I like life. I have my love of nature, my friends, my enjoyment of thought."

Basically, Marvin is an optimist. He is happy, he says, because he has learned to lower his expectations. "I don't expect life to give me a charge every half hour. I feel lucky to be alive. A lot of people weren't even born! And a lot of those who *were* had a very rough time and died early on.

"It's like party crashing. Some places you are not invited, but once there, you avail yourself of every opportunity. I didn't ask to be born, yet here I am. So I try to take advantage."

Marvin Cohen smiled, pleased with his analogy, and took another sip of Chablis.

Photo by Tim Green, *The Tatler*, June 10th 1989

Marvin Cohen is the author of fifteen published books: four novels, a book on baseball, eight collections of short pieces and two poetry anthologies.

His shorter work has appeared in over 100 magazines and books, including: *Ambit, Antaeus, Assembling, Center Magazine, Cricket Addict's Archive, Essaying Essays, Extensions, Harper's Bazaar, Hudson Review, Monk's Pond, The Nation, National Camp Director's Guide, New Directions in Prose and Poetry, The New York Times, Plays from the New York Shakespeare Festival, The Pushcart Prize, Quarterly Review of Literature, Salmagundi, Sun and Moon, Transatlantic Review, The Village Voice, Vogue (UK)*, and *Wormwood Review*.

His writing ranges from the experimental to fable; from poetry to prose; from internal dialogues to playscripts; from art criticism to cricket fandom; from humour to philosophical essays, and from aesthetics to surrealism (he says "if people say so then it must be true").

His 1980 play *The Don Juan and the Non-Don Juan* was first performed at the New York Shakespeare Festival as part of the *Poets at the Public Series*. Staged readings of the play have featured actors Wallace Shawn, Richard Dreyfuss, Keith Carradine, Jill Eikenberry and Mimi Kennedy.

Born in Brooklyn in 1931, Cohen has described himself as one who has "risen from lower-class background to lower-class foreground." He studied art at Cooper Union but left college to focus on writing, supporting himself with a series of odd jobs, from mink farmer to merchant seaman. He later taught creative writing at various New York colleges, including The New School, the City College of New York and Adelphi University.

For a long time, Marvin Cohen has lived in the Lower East Side, New York City, with his wife Candace.